Can't Let Go

A.A Schenna

Cover Art:
Michelle Crocker

http://mlcdesigns4you.weebly.com/

Publisher's Note:

This is a work of fiction. All names, characters, places, and events are the work of the author's imagination.

Any resemblance to real persons, places, or events is coincidental.

Solstice Publishing - www.solsticepublishing.com

Can't Let Go
By A.A Schenna

DEDICATION
To my mother, the best present God has given me so far

Life is a song - sing it. Life is a game - play it. Life is a
challenge - meet it. Life is a dream - realize it. Life is a
sacrifice - offer it. Life is love - enjoy it.
Sai Baba

Are You Lonesome Tonight?

R alph looked at his wife and smiled. He loved seeing his partner sleeping next to his side, breathing peacefully. He had missed the feeling of having his beloved fiancé in the bed, touching her skin, smelling her perfume, feeling the warmth of her body on his.

He rolled his eyes and thanked God for everything. He stretched out his arms and covered her back with the blue sheet, still admiring her tight, naked body. Ralph was thrilled; his facial expression made him seem like a little boy who had the chance to get the best present ever. The glow in his big eyes, his bright smile and trembling hands kept exposing the joy he felt. The nightmare had come to an end and he couldn't find the appropriate words to describe the relief. Ralph had finally found the road to love again and he was sure that his partner would never leave their home. No, she would never do this again.

The tall man got up from the bed and the moonlight showed off his muscular body. He put on his clothes and gazed at his partner, feeling calm and confident, ready to accept the challenges of life. Sonya was still sleeping, but she looked wonderful and relaxed. She was not in danger anymore. The way she breathed and the smile on her face made Ralph think of the past. The night reminded him of the girl he had first met and had fallen in love.

He touched his chin and kept admiring her beauty. He had made it; he'd gotten his girl back, all of her. He had found Sonya he knew back.

The woman of his dreams shook her head and smiled as her eyelids covered the mirrors of her soul. Sonya had finally gotten over her paleness and now, the light tan color had returned back on her sweet face again.

"Where are you going?" she whispered.

"I want to see her, I want to make sure she is fine,"

Ralph said and sat down next to her, pulling her long hair back.

"I'm sure she is, everything is good, honey," she said and locked her gaze on him.

It was like calling him to stay in bed, sharing more erotic moments. Sonya bit her lips and licked them, enticing him to stay.

"Give me a second," Ralph murmured and left the spacious, white room.

"Okay," Sonya said and laughed, watching his steps.

Ralph came back and closed the door behind him, rushing to take off his white shirt and pants. His partner couldn't take her eyes off him. She nodded at Ralph, and pulled the sheet aside as he came near and lay down next to her.

"I missed you so much," he said as Sonya felt unable to respond. She looked up and tried to seal the moment in her mind. She had missed caressing his hair and smelling his aftershave.

Ralph kept spreading his kisses across her beautiful skin, increasing her desire to feel his body on hers. Her lovely feet and her well-shaped curves had managed to stir up his erotic mood and he couldn't resist.

"I will always love you," Sonya whispered and held him tight.

"I will always love you too," Ralph said and lay on her, making his partner ready to scream. She loved the moments he used to conquer her body. She regarded Ralph was the best lover she had ever had. Her partner had found the way to steal her thoughts and soul, making her eager to have sex with him.

Sonya flushed and caught his head, holding it firmly but tenderly. The moment Ralph looked into her eyes; she rested her hands on his back and looked impatient to steal his kisses. She loved biting softly his lips; she adored having him in bed, seducing her mind and her body. Ralph had found the way to drive her crazy and knew how to make her lose her mind. And he was the man who would do anything for her. He would never betray her trust and her heart.

They made love again. Every kiss, every touch, every look was precious and they would never sacrifice the feeling of making love to each other again.

"I want a boy," Sonya confessed. Ralph smiled.

"Don't laugh at me!" Sonya said and laughed.

"Are you sure you are ready? Do you think you could handle the pressure?" Ralph asked.

"Yes, I'm pretty sure, Ralph."

The air of relief and the moonlight kept invading the room as the sweat didn't stop running down their naked bodies. They made love all night, trying to get back the time they had lost. Their adventure was over and they were both ready to move on with their life together. They were both looking forward to adding a new member in their family. But, despite their efforts, they had to wait.

Five years later, they welcomed their son.

They had a beautiful family. They had a beautiful home.

Desert Roses

S hania pulled her blonde hair back and struggled to escape from the memories of the past.

"What are you thinking?" Ryan asked.

"Nothing…" Shania said as she tried to remain calm.

The teenage girl half-closed her eyes and hid her face behind the magazine she held. She walked to the living room and fought back tears. She wanted to avoid becoming emotional since she would destroy her brother's mood and she thought she didn't have the right to hurt him.

Shania was seventeen while Ryan was only twelve. It was their first weekend away from their home, and although they both loved their grandparents, they would never feel like they felt before.

Shania sank in the brown sofa and looked outside the large door of the spacious living room. She could see the grass; she could smell the white roses as her mind flooded with the beautiful pictures of the past when the family used to admire the flowers, the colorful roses, and the beautiful trees of the big house.

The photos of her parents above the white fireplace stole her attention and gave birth to optimism. *"No matter what, don't stop hoping,"* her parents loved telling her. Shania would never forget their smiles; they always loved talking and having fun with their children.

"Tell me something I don't know." Ryan sat down next to his sister and gazed upon her big eyes.

"Let me think," Shania whispered and changed her mood.

The teenage girl smiled at her brother and hugged him tight whereas she didn't stop thinking of a true sign of love from their family to make her brother admire and appreciate those who brought them to life.

"I want to know everything. Next time we'll see them, I'm going to tell them I know anything," Ryan said while Shania nodded and agreed. She wouldn't leave him to flirt with pain and questions. Then again, she decided to let herself free since the tears started running down her face, but she didn't care. Besides, her brother couldn't see her eyes anymore. He was locked in her arms and he felt safe. He believed things would get better and the family would overcome everything.

"I'll tell you and then we'll go outside. It's a beautiful day and we shouldn't miss it! I think we should go to the pool and swim. California is perfect. We should enjoy the good weather and the high temperatures." Shania sounded happy; she wanted to encourage her brother.

"That's awesome!" Ryan said, locked in his sister's hug.

***

School was over and Ryan loved summer, swimming in the large pool, and of course Saturday walks along with their grandparents. But he also wanted to know everything concerning their parents.

On the other hand, Shania would have to think of her studies and her future. She would go to college and she had had to focus on her interests. This summer she would have to think of everything.

"How do you know that? Who told you?" their grandmother asked and stared at Shania.

"What do you mean, Grandma?" Shania stretched out her legs and sat comfortably in the sofa. Her tight blue jeans and the white T-shirt made her look like her mother. Then again, his blue athletic attire and messy black hair made Ryan look like his father.

"Who told you?" the aged woman asked Shania again and sat down in the brown chair opposite Ryan and Shania.

"My mother," Shania answered vaguely.

The woman rolled her eyes and shook her head. She took a deep breath and Shania's words reminded her of the most critical moments she and her son had ever lived.

"Do you remember, Grandma?" Ryan asked and waited for an answer.

He fixed his eyes on the woman with the black clothes and the pale face. She was about sixty years old and she was in great shape. She looked fabulous for a woman in her age.

"Yes, I do, Ryan," she said and smiled.

"Tell us." Ryan sounded impatient.

"Yes, Grandma, tell us," Shania whispered and nodded at the aged woman.

"Okay."

The woman started talking while Ryan focused his sight on his grandmother.

Shania looked down and wished she had the power to turn back time. She wasn't able to hear anything and anyone. Whenever she looked for peace and serenity, she could stay away from reality, living in her own microcosm.

Shania loved making dreams. She hoped she would find someone special like her father, someone who would know what love means.

Chapter One

H e knew he had to accept the fact that he would never see her again. He knew that he had to be strong. He had to pull himself back together.

As he was trying to make the baby calm, Ralph realized that nothing would be the same again. He half-closed his eyes and tried to catch his breath. His daughter had turned red as she didn't stop crying and glancing at the cramped room, looking for her mother.

The moment Shania fell asleep again, he came across reality. Ralph took a few steps and stood in front of the small window. After a while, he placed his hands on the cold glass and gazed at the reflection as he wished he would get past the nightmare.

Ralph looked back and saw his baby sleeping and, immediately, he felt weird. The absurd fate had broken the rules of harmony and, in a flash, he ran into the worst experience of his life.

Although his baby had stopped crying and he breathed the air of relief, he knew that he was trapped in the zone of vagueness and could do nothing to get away. He couldn't stop biting his lips and looking outside the window. He kept shaking as he was not eager to come closer to the path of the ruthless reality. The warm, beautiful home had turned into a silent house where nothing reminded him of the sweet, carefree moments of the past. This place was not his precious shelter anymore.

Out of the blue, Ralph shook his head and started smiling since he wanted to avoid the dangerous games of his mind. His partner had managed to bring him face-to-face with the worst fact of his life, but it was not the time to deal with her unexpected reaction. Ralph was struggling to survive as he wasn't able to think of anything other than his daughter's future. "Oh gosh, if only I could change things," he kept whispering.

The memories of the past came up and flooded his mind and his soul. "This can't be true," he murmured.

He assumed that he had to forget her and move on his life, focusing on his baby, but it was too soon for anything other than trying to escape from the freaking nightmare.

Ralph placed his hands on his face and tried to prevent the tears from making their appearance, and to be optimistic as well, but his partner's naïve action, the secrets and the lies Sonya had decided to put in their lives -- destroying their relationship- -didn't help him find the hope he was looking for.

The night had dressed the whole city while the dark thoughts had enveloped his mind driving him toward the road to insanity. Everything fought against his serenity and, soon, he would start losing control. Although Ralph was determined to overcome the new, dangerous challenge in his life, he couldn't ignore the possibilities of his success. He felt stranded in the zone of hopelessness, and it was obvious that he needed help. Ralph kept walking around in the small room thinking of the reason his partner had left their home.

Ralph would never leave his child. He wanted to believe that things would get better, but he was living a hell and he had to find the mother of his baby as well. He had decided to focus on his child and no matter how harshly his partner and life had treated him, he knew that he had to adjust to reality and deal with the tragedy. It would be very difficult to move on, but he had to ignore her betrayal and make a new beginning.

He sat in the chair gazing at his baby and, before long, the strong wind made him get his life back. The moment he heard the branches of the large sycamores leaning toward the yellow tile roof, he assumed she came back home and started smiling. In a flash, his shoulders loosened and made him look peaceful and happy as usual. He was looking forward to hearing her footsteps on the white tile floor and seeing her lovely eyes again.

Ralph took a deep breath and then swept the tears away from his face. He had locked his sight on the white door and waited for Sonya.

After several minutes, he froze in fear again, losing the hope he was striving to maintain. *She is gone,* he thought and, immediately, he began flirting with anger, disappointment, and depression. Ralph squeezed his hands on the chair's arms and felt the need to expose his inner feelings. He wanted to scream, he wanted to break everything he could see.

Instead, he bit his lips and wished he could turn back the time and avoid meeting her since Sonya had invaded his world and had never respected his trust and honest behavior.

Ralph looked around him and realized everything was in vain. He needed time to get used to the fact that she had dumped them while he had to stop making dreams for the future. He was sure their relationship was nothing more than a tragic theme in the theater of life. He believed that she was an excellent actress while he was just an untalented artist who served as her greatest fan. Ralph would do anything for her to see her happy.

He stood up and walked to the door as the tears kept running down his face. He looked behind him and his eyes rested on his precious baby, thinking of the night she came into their world. "We will be together now, I promise I will never leave you," he mumbled and nodded in affirmation.

Ralph looked around him and gazed at the desk where he could see the first photo with their baby in his embrace. His partner's smile stole his attention. He placed his fingers on the photo and admired her glow in silence, wondering about the wonderful times they had spent together. He leaned his head against the pink wall and turned off the lights. *Why did she do that?* He kept considering as he couldn't explain absurd fate.

His daughter was sleeping while he kept watching her in silence, thinking of the carefree moments of their life. Ralph looked as cold and lifeless as a statue. He was helpless and hoped he would find someone to hold his hand and reassure him that things would get better.

The sweet memories of the past came up again. Everything seemed the same as the first night they had brought their daughter home. *"Keep your voice down; you will wake her up,"* he had told his partner while doing his best to put their baby in the bed without annoying her.

That night Ralph was so happy that he couldn't control his feelings; he was smiling all the time and he loved kissing and caressing Sonya's face.

Ralph adored both his partner and his baby and he would die for them. Pure feelings carried on flooding their hearts and souls, making them realize the real meaning of life. Ralph had everything he wanted, everything he had dreamed of.

The night they welcomed the new member of their family into their home he didn't sleep. He was the happiest man on earth. Now, he was the most miserable man on the planet and he felt ready to collapse. His legs were trembling. The reflection in the large, round mirror showed someone who was looking for sympathy and help. There was a young, helpless man wearing black jeans, a grey sweater, having messy hair and big, sad eyes, begging for mercy. He really looked like a sorrowful angel who was in desperate need of support.

Ralph felt he was cursed and couldn't stop thinking about the consequences of destiny, impulsiveness and love at first sight. He believed that someone, for unknown reasons, had decided to destroy his life by stealing his partner's mind, tearing down their future. Ralph was sure that fate had decided to attack to ruin the plans and the dreams of a lifetime. In a flash, he had lost his entire world.

The lovely memories of the happy past haunted his mind again but, in no time, Sonya's betrayal crossed his thinking and dangerous illusions took over.

Ralph glanced at the reflection again and smiled. Suddenly he had the perception that he could actually sense Sonya's presence in the adorable, pink room of their daughter. Moreover, he was certain she was standing next to him, caressing his back and his head. He could smell her perfume. "Oh my God, I miss you so much," he confessed.

Out of the blue Shania started crying and he came back to reality. Ralph took a few steps and stood above her small, pink bed. The young man watched his baby, admiring her beauty, her energy and the need to feel safe. He placed his elbows on his daughter's bed and surrendered to the wonderful scent of his baby, which kept spreading through the small room.

Ralph had heard many people saying that babies could help you overcome everything --since they have the ability to expel the negative energy-- and, now, he could confirm that their theory was true.

He felt calm as if nothing had taken place in the house, but his daughter needed her mother and she had to feel secure to remain quiet. A glimpse toward her mother would be enough to help her get her stillness back.

The moment Ralph held his daughter in his hands, he felt wonderful; it was like coming across pure love. Shania's presence made him flirt with optimism since her sweet face and her big, blue eyes helped him get past the depression and the consequences of her mother's crazy actions. His daughter was the best thing that had ever happened to him and, regardless of the fact that he had only known her for three months; he swore that this love would last forever. He spent all the time he could with her. He loved reading her tales and watching her doing her magic tricks with her tiny lips and her beautiful fingers.

Ralph kissed her head and, then, the tears stopped running down her lovely, red cheeks. He took Shania in his arms and placed her beautiful, tiny fingers in his hand, dancing the rhythm of love. When he started singing, his daughter looked upon him, she smiled and, after a while, she began making those magnificent grimaces, struggling to communicate with him. Ralph was sure that if she could talk, she would ask a question about her mother and the reason she wasn't there.

Shania wanted to talk, she kept looking around her and Ralph betted that she missed her mother.

Before seeing his baby upset again, he laughed and kissed her forehead, sensing her relief covering his pale face, Ralph felt unable to resist smelling her scent. He adored her smell—it was the scent of an angel.

Every time Ralph held this tiny human being in his arms, nothing could prevent positive thoughts from dominating his mind. He used to wait breathlessly, watching for every single move she made.

The baby meant everything to him. Shania was his treasure and he was determined to do everything he could to make her happy. His daughter's happiness would become the main purpose of his entire life and nothing would stop him from achieving his goal.

Surprisingly, Ralph began making plans as the atmosphere of his baby's room, her tiny clothes and her photos changed entirely his mood. When he fixed his eyes on her, he realized that he hadn't lost everything yet. He might have done the worst mistake by sharing his first love with an introverted mysterious woman, but he would never regret having a baby in his early twenties.

A few minutes later Shania fell asleep again and he smiled. He kept looking at her while thinking of their future, ignoring the presence of her mother in their lives. But he had to find out what had caused her exit from their home.

***

Ralph left his baby's room and walked toward the white bedroom since he had to discover the reason Sonya had decided to abandon them. He opened the door and his eyes focused on her things. Then, he took a few steps and stood in front of the large mirror, trying to remember their last moments together.

Soon, he realized that he couldn't even look at the reflection because he hated the way he had been treated. He felt naïve, humiliation wrapped up his confidence. Nothing could remind him of something that he might have done to make her leave everything behind and seek something else. He was certain that there was no serious reason to dump him and of course their sweet baby.

Ralph tried very hard to remain calm and avoided thinking of the worst scenarios since he hadn't discovered the most tragic fact of his life yet.

When he heard the sound of his cell phone, he froze, paralyzed in fear and agony. He was afraid to get the black device in his hands, he hesitated; he was not ready to deal with the worst experience of his life.

"We are fine, Mom, everything is great." He caught his breath and sat down on the chair. Later, he got up and lay on his bed while he kept talking with his mother, trying to retain his composure.

"That's great, I am so happy for you," she said.

"Hey, Mom, would you be able to come and help us for a few days?" Ralph sounded happy, as if nothing had happened. Although he needed a shelter to let his soul rest in peace, he didn't have the least intention of confessing anything yet. He touched his chin and half-closed his eyes because he felt guilty. Ralph hated lies and he never liked pretending, hiding facts and the truth from the people he truly loved.

"Of course, honey," his mother said.

While the woman continued telling her son her

news, Ralph gazed at the small desk and got up from the bed. There was no way to believe that she would be back soon since Sonya used to mention her plans and didn't like acting arbitrarily.

Ralph started searching through his partner's things and, soon, he discovered that she hadn't taken the money from the small shelf with her. She'd left three hundred dollars and all the credit cards. Doubts started circling his mind as he strived to get out of the ocean of sorrow.

Sonya had made up her mind, she had left their home, but he had to know the reason she had acted this way. Ralph kept looking for her things while still talking with his mother, and the moment he looked in the closet, he froze in fear. Sonya hadn't taken her bag and her wallet. His partner hadn't taken her cell phone either and, before long, he found out that she had taken nothing with her except her coat and her gloves.

"I will see you tomorrow, Mom," he mumbled.

Ralph placed her wallet on the desk and lay down. He gazed at the ceiling wondering about his next step. It was not the time to confess his problem yet and, besides, his parents would cause him more pain and doubts since they had warned him about his critical decision.

He remembered their words. *"You just finished school, how are you supposed to raise a child?"* they had told him.

That time Ralph thought his parents were insane and he believed they didn't like his girlfriend. But, despite their suggestions and objections, he risked it since he was sure they would make it. He regarded that love was enough to face up everything and, moreover, they would win the battle against all difficulties, heading toward the road to euphoria.

It was great being an optimist, but he had to be more cautious and serious with his decisions as well. Then again, he could never imagine that life would treat him badly and that destiny would have other plans for him. If only he knew...

He sat up abruptly. He needed to take action. Ralph wasted no time. He searched everywhere in the house again and, in a few minutes, he had managed to check out the whole place. He had searched all the rooms but in vain.

Later, he stepped into his daughter's room to see if everything was good and, then, he decided to look for his partner in the basement. She used to complain about the stairs and he wanted to make sure she had no accident.

He searched for her in the attic, then he went outside the house and walked around the neighborhood, but she was nowhere. His effort to find the mother of his child came across failure after failure.

After several minutes Ralph ran back home and stood behind the front door trying to catch his breath. He got in the house and sat in his partner's favorite chair wondering about her action. He sank in the comfortable seat, feeling lost in the place where his happiness was born.

"She left us," he whispered and, finally, he realized that his partner was gone. She had decided to get away from everything and everyone.

***

Ralph went upstairs and moved toward the baby's room because he needed to get his positive energy and optimism back. He had the perception that one glimpse at Shania would be enough to replenish his feelings.

"I love you so much. I promise I will never leave you," he murmured as he leaned against the pink door and crossed his heart.

Shania looked like an angel. His baby was still sleeping while he was trying to find the best way to handle the entire situation.

Ralph took a few steps and headed toward the window where, later, he rested his head on the cold glass and carried on gazing at the snowflakes.

The snow had covered the quiet neighborhood as he watched the beautiful scene in silence, recalling the first moments of their acquaintance.

Although the agony had enveloped his soul and the fear kept running in his veins, he wanted to believe that things would resolve quickly, having a happy ending, of course.

On the other hand, Ralph was a realist. He was afraid that she might not return, maybe she would never come back. He couldn't keep these thoughts from invading and taking over.

Sonya had no reason to ignore the existence of their child. When she first met Ralph, she was sure they would spend the rest of their lives together.

Chapter Two

H er big beautiful eyes carried on staring at the towering pine trees. After a while, Sonya looked up at the sky and the shining stars of the summer night.

Loneliness had decided to settle in her life. She felt the air of liberty covering her pale face until the moment she heard someone opening the door.

The handsome, middle-aged man came into the spacious living room and walked toward the balcony, as it was obvious that Sonya was taken aback. The way she looked back at him made the man eager to speak up without losing time.

"What is this mess?" he asked angrily.

The moments of happiness belonged to the past, and every minute that passed by, depression continued coming closer and closer. He was looking forward to getting rid of the nasty memories; he needed a change. He hated coming across the same scene, and all he wanted was to escape.

She gave no answer, seemingly ignoring him. She took a deep breath and focused on the stars. She would never forgive him.

"I am talking to you!" He walked to her side and stood behind her, but she remained still, her beauty dazzling the silent diamonds in the sky.

Then again, he couldn't take it anymore--he had no more patience. They were both destroying their lives and they had to do something. There was no reason pretending that everything was fine since living together was another freaking nightmare. He was determined not to postpone their discussion, not this time.

"What is this mess?" he asked again.

They both needed time; they hadn't healed the injuries in their souls yet. The carefree, wonderful memories of the past couldn't save their relationship because they had already lost their connection. They had become two strangers living under the same roof.

"What mess are you talking about? I don't understand you." She sounded nervous and didn't look at him.

"I am talking about you! Look at yourself! Stand in front of the mirror and you will understand what I mean."

Sonya turned back, and by the way she looked at him, he seemed worried about her.

"If this is what you want…"

"Yes, this is what I want."

The young woman shook her head and laughed at him.

"Okay."

She came into the house and moved toward the mirror.

"I'm in the mirror," Sonya said.

"What do you see?" He asked.

"I see me! Are you happy now?" She looked like a soulless human being.

"No, I am not!" he answered angrily.

There was nothing left to admire; her big blue eyes had lost their glow since the sorrow had wrapped up her soul. The tragic facts had stolen her energy and she felt helpless, she seemed weak, unable to deal with the challenges of life.

The past would always haunt her thoughts, and as much as she would try, Sonya would never overcome the difficulties of living along with this man, and probably with any other man.

"What do you want from me?" Sonya asked and raised her hands.

Her blonde hair covered her face and hid the tears of hopelessness. Then again, the black clothes made her look like a sorrowful angel. She had become the shadow of her life.

"I want to see the young lady who had dreams. I miss the girl I used to see in the past," he said while he shook his head and tried to make her deal seriously with herself.

Sonya pulled her long hair away from her face and placed her hands on the large mirror. She thought she had to do something, she had to be honest. She ought to speak up.

"You made me look like this," she said, losing her patience, ready to expose her pain. She would not hold back her anger any more, because with every day that passed by, she continued losing herself while coming closer to hell.

"What do you mean?" he asked.

"You are responsible for this, you are responsible for everything," Sonya turned back and gazed at him. She bit her lips and, then, a pained smile appeared on her face.

"I gave you my love, I gave you ..." He had to defend himself.

"Are you sure about that?" she asked.

"Yes!" he shouted.

Sonya shook her head.

"Don't you dare to mention this word again because you have no idea what love means."

When she raised her hand, he panicked and took off his tie. He turned red as she was still angry. Sonya had never crossed the line before and her reaction surprised him. Sonya had turned into a tiger ready to cut off his confidence and belief.

"Now you think that I don't know what love means..." He stepped closer to her. This woman, his daughter, was a stranger to him.

"Yes, you are the last man in the world who could talk about love," Sonya sounded sure about her confession.

Her father unbuttoned his blue shirt and sat in the

white chair, while the tall woman stared at him. She was ready to reveal the dark feelings, although her father was not feeling well. He suffocated; he was in desperate need of some fresh air. But Sonya hadn't forgotten the past and the tragic facts.

The man's sight locked on the painting above the large fireplace and his gaze didn't drop his daughter's sight. After a while, she glanced at the female figure as well, and she started crying.

The woman on the painting looked fabulous. She had blonde hair and wore a long, red dress, but everyone could see her ambiguous grimace. The pained smile on her face was the same as that of Sonya. The young lady looked like her mother.

"I did everything I could to make you happy," her father said, brushing his silver hair away from his eyes.

"You surely made it!" The tears kept running down her pale face.

"This is what I could offer you," he said.

"Congratulations, but you failed!" Sonya shook her head and laughed at him again.

"Do you think I am satisfied? Do you actually think I like this situation?" her father asked.

"You brought the devil in our house," Sonya took a few steps and stood in front of him.

"No, my girl, I did not," he said firmly.

Sonya was not going to make the same mistake again. She knelt, looked upon his sweaty face and, then, she began laughing. It was obvious that she wanted to hurt him.

"You are responsible for everything that took place in this house," she whispered.

"I did nothing wrong," he said.

All these years, Sonya had been living a nightmare. She used to abstain from saying anything that could destroy the fake balance in their life. In her view, the grey-haired man had done nothing to heal the pain in her heart, and

24

instead of being next to her side, he preferred living his life. She'd always believed that her father was indifferent for her feelings.

"Do you really believe that?" she asked.

"Yes, I do," he murmured while Sonya half-closed her eyes and laughed again.

The cheerless woman regarded that he would never stop acting like a teenager. Moreover, she was certain that her father had no idea what love meant to her, and she could bet that he actually didn't care about loyalty. Deep inside her soul Sonya wanted to forgive him, but his attitude couldn't let her do that since his words made her believe that he knew how to betray those who really loved him.

"You see, Father, I believe this is ironic," she said and stood up.

The young woman tried very hard to get past the anger she felt, but she couldn't make it. Although she had everything she had ever dreamed of, she couldn't forget the nasty moments from the past. Sonya had never missed money, expensive clothes and cars, but all these were not enough to make her feel happy and safe since his lack of pure emotions, understanding and communication had ruined their relationship.

"Why is that?" he asked.

"You stole my happiness, Father." Sonya gazed at him and waited for his answer.

"I am responsible for everything. Is this what you really want to hear?" His facial expression triggered her obsession. Her father's face started twitching; he looked ready to cry. On the other hand, it was obvious that Sonya didn't like his behavior. Her eyes became flinty.

"As far as I'm concerned, I believe that you are responsible for everything," she exclaimed.

Sonya waited for many years for this moment, and she wished she would become stronger, ready to deal with everything and everyone.

Her father stood up and walked to her side as his eyes remained locked on hers. He looked like a dead man walking--he was suffering, his daughter was suffering and the pain continued on, increasing with time. But they were not willing to give up on their discussion.

"What did I do, my daughter?" he asked.

"You stole my happiness, Father." Sonya really meant her words.

"No, I did not," her father said.

"Yes, you did," she said and bit her lips.

"I did everything I could to protect you and your brother," he whispered, trying to excuse his behavior.

"I don't believe you," she said.

Sonya's tears shattered his heart and he rushed to hold his daughter in his arms. But Sonya didn't want his hug; it was too late. She pushed him away.

"Why?" he asked.

"Look at me, Father! Look at me!" she demanded. "I am looking at you!" He tried to hug her again but in vain.

"What do you see?" Sonya snapped.

"I see a young girl who has--"

She interrupted him.

"Do you know what I see?" she asked.

"What do you see, my child?" He seemed impatient to hear her answer. He placed his hands on his jaw, waiting.

"I see a young woman who is finally free to get away. Now that it's my turn to leave from this house. I'm ready to go to college, I should be happy, but I look awful and that's because you destroyed me."

"That's not true," Her father swept his tears away, his breathing rapid.

"Yes it is. I'm still a miserable teenage girl, Father, and that's because of you," she said, and that moment, Sonya wanted to slap her father.

They were both tense; they were determined to admit and confess everything they felt because they had no more patience. He couldn't stand seeing his daughter destroying her life, and she couldn't stand living with her father. Sonya hated knowing that she was sharing the same house with the man who had killed her mother. They both couldn't tolerate anything more--they couldn't tolerate one another.

"You betrayed us," Sonya said.

"How did I betray you, Sonya?" her father asked.

"I trusted you; my brother trusted you, and you made both of us feel like fools." In her fury, she couldn't stop accusing her father.

"This is so unfair." Her father walked to the balcony. He needed some fresh air to avoid collapsing in front of his daughter.

"We trusted you!"

"What do you want me to say?" Her father turned back. He had never seen his daughter like this before. Sonya was always distant, ignoring his presence in their house.

"You are a creep and I hate you! You killed my mother!" He rushed to her side and stood in front of her.

"What did you say, Sonya?" her father asked angrily.

"You are a creep. I hate you!" He slapped his daughter and Sonya started crying.

Her father started shaking. Anger and hurt held equal sway with him.

"Thanks, Aston," Sonya laughed. Her father stood in front of the mini-bar. He had never thought that one day his daughter would call him by his first name.

He clutched the bottle of the wine in his hands and, then, he looked upon the large painting. He loved his wife, he really did.

"I loved Erica! She was my wife; she was my love,

the mother of my children," he said.

Aston was not prepared for this conversation, and even though he started it, he could never imagine that he would actually slap his daughter. He kept shaking while struggling to maintain his calmness.

"Which is why you started cheating on her--am I right?" Sonya asked, provoking her father.

"One day you will regret for your words." He sounded certain about his prediction.

Sonya decided to keep her voice down and didn't push it too far. Her mother's loss was the worst experience she had ever lived, but her father was always there for her. Regardless of his countless mistakes, Sonya had never missed his support. Sonya always wanted more, but Aston had a difficult career and a home to look after.

"I didn't kill your mother," her father confessed.

"Do you think you gave Mom love?" Sonya gazed at the beautiful painting and waited for her father's answer.

"I gave her everything she wanted," he said.

"Are you sure about that?" his daughter asked.

"Of course I am sure." Aston sounded nervous.

"Why did she kill herself?" Sonya's eyes hooked on his.

"Your mother was happy with me." The memories came up and circled his mind.

"She used to cry all day and she wore the same black clothes again and again, Dad. Do you really think she was happy? Tell me! Do you think she was happy, Dad? Do you think you gave her love, Dad?" Sonya was relentless with her questions.

"Why are you doing this to me?" Aston asked.

Sonya had waited many years for this moment. She was out of control and nothing could stop her revealing her true feelings about her father. The moment of truth had come, and as it seemed, nothing would be the same again.

"Do you think Mom was happy, Dad?"

"No," Aston said softly.

"Have you ever wondered the reason?" Sonya was acting like a judge. She kept walking around her father like a shark that had managed to trap its victim.

"I..." His eyes pierced hers, and that moment, he seemed ready to confess the last secret.

"Yes, Dad, I'm listening." The truth was almost here.

"I..." Aston was ready to tell her everything about Erica.

An angry voice startled them. "Stop it! Both of you stop it!"

"John!" Sonya was taken aback, as was Aston. Neither had seen him enter.

"Stop it!" her brother repeated.

"No, John, this is not going to happen, not this time," his sister intoned.

Sonya was eager to keep up their conversation since she wouldn't have any other chance to confess her feelings and complaints. The following morning she would leave her house, she would be far away from both of them. Her father along with her older brother would no longer be next to her side. Sonya would be free to move on and live her life the way she wanted.

"Sonya, let's forget about it," John hated seeing them fighting.

"No, John, I'm still in pain," his sister said while seeking for his support.

"All of us are in pain." Aston sounded different and confused. He placed his hands on his chin, thinking of their condition and his daughter's reaction. He worried about Sonya.

"Why are we pretending that nothing has changed, Father?" She was curious about his answer.

Sonya got no answer since both her father and John avoided telling her the truth. No one was able to say something or at least to justify some things.

"Why are you acting like this?" John asked.

"I'm hopeless!" Sonya's tears started running down her pale cheeks.

"Why are you saying that?" John held her hand and tried to comfort his sister.

"Look at me, John!"

Sonya made her father and John remember some horrible moments from the past.

Aston started thinking that he had actually ruined his daughter's life by not telling her the truth, while John was afraid that the nightmare they had lived in that house would come back again. John thought the family's curse had woken up, and this time, no one would survive.

Sonya's behavior brought some ugly memories from the past back to his mind and John didn't like that. His beloved sister reminded him of their mother and everything she had done to all of them.

"I see you," John said vaguely and she looked toward their father.

"What do you see, Father?" Sonya asked.

"I see you, honey." Aston seemed helpless.

"Do you think I'm happy, John?" Sonya sounded like a child.

"No," John said and shook his head.

"I'm glad because Dad thinks I'm happy." Sonya leaned toward her brother's shoulder.

"I didn't say that…" Aston looked at John and, then, they both realized what they were dealing with.

"Did you receive love, John?" Sonya was curious.

"Why are we having this discussion?" John watched his father as he caressed his sister's hair.

"I never received love, John." Sonya left her brother's hug and walked around their father.

"I am sorry, my precious baby," her brother said.

"You are not the one who should say sorry, John,"

Sonya whispered.

The moment Aston tried to hold her in his arms, she pushed him away. At the same time, her brother could clearly understand that nothing could be done to prevent the ghost of the past from setting off. He was sure they were going to live the nightmare of the past again, but this time, the nightmare would haunt their lives forever.

"Is this what you want to hear from me?" Aston asked.

"Yes, Father," Sonya murmured and swept her tears away.

"I am sorry."

"Do you mean it?" she asked.

"What?" Aston was surprised.

"Do you mean it?" Sonya asked again.

"I am…" He felt that his daughter didn't respect anything.

"You are a selfish man."

Sonya raised her eyebrows. John shook his head in disappointment.

"I am a selfish man…" Aston felt that his own daughter had managed to humiliate him.

"You didn't give me love, you gave me poison," she said and stood in front of him.

"I am really sorry." Aston stared at John.

"I'm sorry too, Father."

"Why are you sorry, Sonya?" Aston asked.

"For leaving you and, moreover, for seeing you destroying my life. But I am not going to let this happen anymore."

Sonya went upstairs and left both her father and her brother in the large living room wondering about their future.

"I gave her poison! Did you hear what she told me?" Aston was still shocked.

"Yes, I did." John wasn't surprised. He avoided

looking at his father.

"Can you believe it?" Aston asked.

"Yes, I can." John made a drink while his father remained where he was.

"What are you saying?" His father couldn't understand him.

"You were wrong, Father." John brushed his black hair away from his eyes and turned back.

"You know I had no other option."

"I can't stand any drama, no drama, please. That's enough for me." John left his drink on the bar.

"What do you mean?" His father asked.

"All these years, I stayed here in this house for you. Now, you are alone."

John had spent his life in a house where he had never felt happy. During his teenage years, he had never had someone to love him, someone to reassure him that things would be fine. But after so many tragedies, John had gotten used to that way of life.

"That's great."

Aston stood in front of the large painting, staring at his wife. He remembered the first time the doctor talked to him about her condition. But he never accepted the truth, and he never thought that his daughter could be like her mother as well.

Did I actually love my wife, my family? He started wondering.

Aston spent the rest of the night going through the family photo albums and gazing at the painting. He really missed the carefree moments of the past. But, the following morning, everything would change.

***

The moment Aston noticed the sun's rays on the balcony; he stretched out his arms and stood up from the sofa. He wished he could smile and enjoy the sunny day like he used to do in the past, but he knew he had to stop having illusions as well.

Aston took a few steps and, before long, he was taken aback.

"That was it," his daughter said.

Sonya appeared from nowhere and managed to surprise him.

"What do you mean?" her father asked.

"I'm leaving forever." Sonya sounded sure about her announcement.

"Are you certain about that?" Aston remained cool.

"It's the first time I'm sure I'm doing the right thing." She turned away.

"I love you." Her father went closer and tried to hug his daughter, but Sonya stepped back.

"Save it."

She put on her sunglasses, and the moment she turned back, John was there. He opened his arms and hugged her tight.

"I love you so much, Sonya." John said.

"I love you too, John," Sonya whispered.

"Try not to forget us." Her brother's voice was strained.

"I will not forget you, John." For once more, she had managed to let her father down.

"Take care," John said.

Sonya closed the front door of their house behind her and headed toward her car. After a while, she stood in front of the black jeep and took off her sunglasses. In a flash she recalled everything she had lived in that house.

Sonya took a deep breath and the lovely memories of the past came up, for an instant overwhelming all the bad things she had experienced.

"You can call us whenever you want, everything you need," her father said.

Aston was outside the house.

"Goodbye," she whispered.

Sonya brushed her blonde hair away from her face and swept the tears away. It was the time to pull herself back together. It was the time to live her life.

Chapter Three

The first time Ralph ran into Sonya, he thought she was the most beautiful woman he had ever seen. He gazed at her sweet face and wished he would have the time to lock her look in his mind forever. Although he always found it easy to flirt with girls, it was the first time he seemed hesitant since he was hiding behind the trunks of the big trees wondering about her reaction. He was afraid that she would let him down. Sonya was fabulous and he thought she would abstain from giving him her number, a chance to meet her or a date.

It was love at first sight, and even though he had never met her before, Ralph felt he could do anything for her. He fell for her immediately, and he was sure he would always remain in love with her big eyes and her wonderful smile.

Sonya had the whole package she was beautiful, smart and loved being independent. The very first impression remained incredible. The moment he gazed at her sweet face, he realized she was everything he was looking for.

Ralph was shaking and couldn't stop twitching as he had already turned red and looked like a young man who was suffering from a fever, which kept increasing. Love and enthusiasm had turned into huge flames of fire, which had wrapped his heart and were ready to burn his body.

***

"I'm Ralph," he said, so low he could hardly hear his own voice.

"I'm Sonya," she said and smiled at him, making Ralph feel confident and hope that their acquaintance would drive them somewhere close to the paradise they both looked for.

Sonya pulled her beautiful, blonde hair away from her face and, then, he stared at her big, blue eyes, feeling grateful to God for giving him the chance to admire her glow.

Sonya was fabulous. She filled every place in his thoughts.-He could smell her perfume and could still hear her sweet voice in his head, making dreams and plans for the forthcoming days, weeks, months and years.

The moment they shook hands, he started feeling weird. She looked like a princess while he was pretty sure that he looked like a nerd. *Why didn't I wear my white shirt and my blue jeans,* he thought, guessing that she kept talking with him because she was feeling sorry for him. But he got over the insecurities since Sonya seemed to enjoy his unanticipated company.

"So, what are you studying?" she asked.

"I always wanted to become a lawyer but, now, I'm not sure if this is what I want to do for the rest of my life. How about you, what are you studying?" He was trembling. He wanted to be cool and find out everything he could about her, but he was extremely nervous too.

"Creative writing, but I'm a bit confused like you and everyone else in this place," Sonya said with a little laugh as she waved her hands and gestured at the countless students walking around them.

Ralph believed she was funny and her answer along with her gesture made him laugh, while Sonya smiled at him again and helped him get his courage back.

"I think we both need some coffee," Ralph said, waiting for her answer.

"I guess you are right," she said. Sonya put on her sunglasses and they began walking toward the library.

She looked like a professional model since her long, black dress and her black heels showed off her natural beauty, becoming the most challenging temptation for the male students.

Sonya was a tall woman and well proportioned, making the majority of the female students feel jealous of her. She was perfect, and, in no time, she had managed to steal everyone's attention. All the students were hooked by her presence and could do nothing but admire her beauty.

On the other hand, Ralph looked like a teenage athlete who would keep seeking for a ball for the rest of his life, ignoring priorities, studies and his career. He looked thirsty for games, jokes and fun with his friends as he didn't stop teasing those he knew. His black, faded pants and his black jacket along with the black sneakers made him look like the most immature person on the planet. But fortunately, he was saved; he had fixed his hair and he kept spreading his positive energy through the whole place. After all, he had done something great--he had dared to talk to the most beautiful girl on campus and had-suggested they should drink a coffee together to talk about their studies. And she'd accepted!

During the carefree stroll, Sonya seemed distant and a little anxious. She avoided looking straight at Ralph. It was like being trapped in a veil of mystery and Ralph wanted to see if he would dig out the secrets of her life.

"Where are you from?" she asked, looking down. "I'm from California. Where are you from?" Ralph asked nervously.

"I'm from Chicago," Sonya whispered.

"I love snow," Ralph said while Sonya continued walking next to him.

"Me too..." Sonya pulled her hair back and didn't say anything else.

After visiting the large library, they went to the small café and sat in the comfortable chairs, feeling ready to step into the adult world. The sun's rays and Sonya's presence had turned a usual day into the best day of Ralph's life. Out of the blue, beautiful emotions wrapped up his soul and his thoughts and, while they were talking about serious matters and about their studies, he couldn't stop smiling. He remained anxious and wished he would have another chance to see her again.

The college was full of curious students like Sonya and Ralph, and everyone seemed to wonder about the future and their critical decisions. Ralph could bet there was no one there who really knew what to do or what to study.

Books, notes, bags, pencils, laptops and of course countless unanswered questions had the main role during the first day at college, and all the students remained anxious, struggling to hide the silent worries behind their pained smiles while observing the changes which had taken place in the theater of their lives. It was like living childhood again, like turning back the time to the first day at school, but there was a serious difference because this time, the new adults would be responsible for the way their futures would evolve. They had stepped into the world of the adults and they were entering the most productive years of their lives.

They had finally made it; they would decide for whatever they wanted. It was their first step to become independent and responsible. They had the right to choose the way of life they desired.

Countless boys and girls kept searching for the classes, the dorms and the teachers, causing an unstoppable, if low key, chaos. Everyone was able to see huge boxes in the halls, numerous visitors, parents and grandparents who didn't stop strolling in the beautiful area feeling proud of the younger members of their families and many more.

As time passed by, the noise carried on increasing while the seniors continued answering questions and were doing their best to help the students from the other states of the country who had never visited the sleepless city adjust to reality by guiding them everywhere it was needed.

In truth, it was like participating at the strangest party ever, but Ralph was having a great time. And so was

Sonya.

"I guess I will see you again." Sonya looked at Ralph and it was obvious that he didn't want her to leave. Ralph was trying to say something; he desired to earn some more time and kept shaking her hand like a small child.

"Yes." He sounded cool, he released her hand, but his inner feelings were ready to scream since all he wanted was to beg her to stay a little bit longer.

"It was nice meeting you, Ralph," Sonya said with a little laugh.

She got up from her comfortable seat and so did Ralph. They shook hands for a last time and then she headed toward her car as he remained steady and breathless, watching every step she took. Finally, when Sonya got into the black jeep, Ralph started breathing normally again, thinking of her last words. But he wasn't sure if she really meant the fact that she liked meeting him. *Yes, sometimes men have insecurities too,* he thought, as he wondered about the absence of his confidence.

Although he sensed that something was wrong with the beautiful girl, Ralph felt ready to risk everything. He could wait for her forever because she had already managed to seduce his mind.

Ralph had noticed the sorrow into her big eyes and had realized that she needed time and patience to replace the pained smile with laughter, but he was impressed by her personality and her image. She was the One. His One.

***

The following morning Ralph saw Sonya sitting on the grass under the shadow of the large pine tree and he did nothing other than admire her. She looked like an angel who had come down to earth to make Ralph's life better.

Sonya was reading a book while her long hair was playing with the wind, teasing his mind and his carefree thoughts. She wore a white t-shirt and blue jeans while her white shoes along with her silver bracelets and rings made her seem like a nymph who was lost in a world where she needed someone to protect her and guide her to the paths of love.

Ralph rushed to meet her, ignoring the fact that she might have needed her privacy. When he reached the place she had decided to rest, he believed he had just made the most terrible mistake since her facial expression showed off the mystery, which kept rising, making her seem different, distant and more attractive as well.

Although Ralph was determined to act dynamic and confident, he rushed headlong into hesitation and embarrassment. When he stared at her pale face, he froze and stepped back. Sonya looked sad and he assumed that she liked being there alone reading her book.

Ralph looked around him and realized that everything was much more different than the previous day. During the first moments at college, everyone was panicked, but the second day things had started getting better since the students were focused on their futures, their studies and the wild parties, of course.

"Hi," he whispered.

"Hi, Ralph." Sonya smiled at him and got up.

Ralph was ready to stretch out his arm and offer his hand, but she managed to disarm his anxiety. Sonya came closer and kissed him. In a flash, Ralph turned red and tried to be cool, while the moment he looked into Sonya's blue eyes, he could tell that she really loved his reaction. Ralph was sure that if she had kissed his lips, he would fall down dead and she would have to call out for someone to help her bring him back to life. Ralph was sure he would have a heart attack.

He leaned against the trunk of the huge tree and the pink clouds of love appeared around and over his head since he dreamed of becoming her boyfriend. Although he knew her only a few hours, he was almost ready to confess that he was in love with her eyes, her smile and the rest divine parts of her being. That moment he wished she would stay with him forever.

"How was your day?" Sonya asked.

"Fine, how was yours?" Ralph asked, trying to be nonchalant.

"I'm still not sure about creative writing." Sonya sounded anxious; she was confused and she needed someone's opinion.

"Let me tell you a secret. I think I don't want to become a lawyer," Ralph said and then she laughed.

"Will you let me buy you a coffee?" he asked.

"Yes." Sonya put the book in her bag and followed him.

***

They discussed future plans, they talked about their dreams and, a few hours later, Ralph believed that he had learned everything about Sonya. He now knew that she was not just a beautiful woman since Sonya was the most interesting person he had ever met. She was aware of books, politics and even sports. She loved baseball and all kinds of music too.

It was only the second day they had spent together and he was pretty sure that Sonya was the one, the special one. Ralph was absolutely certain that Sonya was the girl he was waiting for.

"Do you have any plans for tonight?" He sounded confident when he shouldn't.

Sonya's blue eyes locked on his and, before long, Ralph felt breathless and weak. He couldn't speak, he couldn't breathe and he couldn't even swallow. Her gaze made him freeze; she could affect his body language and play with his patience.

I screwed up everything, Ralph thought as he was sure that he had destroyed his future by rushing to get her and, now, he waited patiently like a beggar for an answer while, at the same time, she did nothing other than staring at his pale face.

The following minutes Ralph felt like a criminal who had done something awful and Sonya's stance reminded him of the movies he liked seeing where criminals used to stand in front of a judge without saying anything while an unknown person would define the rest of their lives.

Ralph assumed that he had scared her. *I shouldn't have asked her going out with me yet. She doesn't even know me,* he kept thinking and wished he would turn back time and take back his proposal and everything else he had said.

"You seem a nice guy and you are handsome. I like your messy black hair and your green eyes, but..." Sonya bit her lips and gazed at him in silence while he was thrilled--at least she liked him.

"We will do whatever you want," Ralph smiled and crossed his heart, making her smile and think seriously about his idea.

Sonya looked into his eyes again and, a few seconds later, she laughed and nodded at him since she knew she could trust him.

On the other hand, Ralph realized that he had to calm her; he had to be funny to reassure her that he would never hurt her feelings and he also wanted to make her sure that he was a nice guy and that she was in no danger.

"I don't even know you," Sonya whispered, but she couldn't say no as well.

"I will not hurt you. I just want to be with you," Ralph chose to be honest and, as time passed by, he found out that he had made the right move. Now, Sonya had no reason to refuse.

"Okay."

When he heard the magic word coming out from her well-shaped lips through her sweet voice, Ralph became the happiest man on earth.

They were both based in New York City and knew no one else there. A few days ago they were two strangers, but ready to discover the center of the world as well. Furthermore, they looked forward to discovering themselves as they were thirsty to run into love. They were impatient to coming across new experiences. They were both curious about sex and they couldn't stop wondering about the advantages and the disadvantages of being in a relationship. They wanted to find out everything.

"You made the right choice," Ralph said with a little laugh.

"I'm sure I can trust you."

That moment he believed she had already become his girlfriend; he thought they would share the rest of their lives together.

"I'm here to protect you, my queen," he said and he really meant every word he confessed.

Then again, Sonya turned red while he held tight to her hands.

Their crazy adventure, their strange story had just started.

Chapter Four

A fter leaving her house and while driving to New York, Sonya had the chance to think of everything that had taken place in her life.

***

Her mother's loss was the most painful thing her family had ever experienced. It was also the strangest fact that had ever happened in the beautiful neighborhood. Everyone was curious about Sonya's mother death since there were many rumours about her behaviour, but none had the guts to say something straight to Aston, John or Sonya.

The residents of the north, rich suburbs of the city knew there was something going on with the wealthy family, but everybody refrained from asking questions. They thought the famous doctor had everything under control and they had never imagined that his wife would commit suicide. Everyone used to be friendlier with the members of the family. They shook hands and were eager to invite them for dinner or coffee, but they loved whispers and gossip as well.

After her mother's funeral, Sonya changed her behaviour and her way of life and, as time passed by, she continued acting strangely. She stayed in her room, complaining about everything, and she didn't want anyone touching her.

At the same time, the despair kept spreading through their house while hopelessness had covered up her soul. The tears, the dry, pale skin, and the black attire had become her best friends. The sighs had replaced the words and she never talked. Besides, for a couple of weeks, no one in her house talked. Every one of them looked sad, austere and silent, ignoring the needs of the family and the fact that they should be united to overcome the depression the unexpected death had caused.

Sonya couldn't stand living with her father. It was very difficult for her to be around to him; she was not ready to join his emotional protection, no, not yet. Sonya preferred hiding at her room listening to music and reading romantic novels than coming closer to her father and John.

The young girl was living her worst nightmare since she had lost her mother, her best friend, her only support. Without her mother's presence, Sonya always felt lifeless and helpless. Most times she looked like a soulless doll dressed in mourning.

Then again, during the most difficult period of her life, Sonya rejected the importance of school. She hated it and the day hours she was living a hell. Everybody in the class thought she was crazy as she wore the same black clothes all the time while the majority of the students never stopped teasing her. "You are a monster, you will suicide like your mother," they used to tell her. But, fortunately, Sonya would find her peace a couple of months later.

Sonya was a lucky girl and got rid of the school problems easily because she was beautiful. The moment she realized the power of her weapon, she got past the spoiled kids. Soon, bullying turned into ash; she became the most popular girl and that was not startling since she looked like a professional model. A few months after her tragic loss, Sonya replaced her sneakers with high heels while the faded pants had been replaced by tight bright blue and red jeans. She didn't wear shirts and jackets anymore. She loved small t-shirts and beautiful colors.

Sonya had discovered the way to set fire to the rain. She used to dare--she was different and she was a smart girl with an excellent appearance. She fought against her fears and liked being social. But, at home, she was acting like a little girl who needed emotional stability.

In the meantime, Aston along with her brother looked helpless as they both found it very difficult to realize they would never see Erica again.

John missed his mother, but he had to be strong for his father and his sister as well. "You are twenty five years old, John, while your sister is only fifteen. Please take care of her and be there for her until you see her strong." He would never forget Erica's last words. He would never forget the moment he saw his mother on the bed, holding all those pills, the pills that stole her life and took her far away from their home.

According to John's silent belief, his father had managed to destroy their family. He regarded that Aston should have done something other to protect them.

As time passed by, John tried very hard to put out of his mind the bad memories, and he would never confess his true feelings to his father.

***

Sonya was in desperate need of a coffee and decided to stop for a while. She swept the tears away and decided to leave the sadness and everything terrible behind. A few minutes later, she got in her car again, heading toward the freeway where she would reconsider her opinion about her father and her brother.

***

"It's my fault," Aston murmured as he regarded that he was responsible for their desperate emotional situation.

"It's not your fault, Father--it was destiny. Please believe me, it's not your fault!" His father sounded awful; John could hardly bear to hear his voice.

John tried to comfort his father; he hugged him tight and, later, he helped him lay down on the sofa. He had never seen Aston like this before. The middle-aged man was shaking. His father had lost his energy, his optimism, and his hope; he was falling apart.

On the other hand, John was striving to make his father feel relieved by standing next to his side, sacrificing his own needs to assist his father.

John had decided to adjust to reality and face up their problems. He didn't deal with the past since he knew that he could do nothing to change things.

"It's my fault. I used to ignore your mother's feelings because I didn't want to understand the way she felt. It's why she reacted the way she did," Aston cried out.

"Don't do this to yourself, stop thinking about it!" His son didn't give up.

John was determined to make him realize that his mother's reaction wasn't his fault, although deeply inside his mind and soul, there were still many unanswered questions.

Actually, his son believed it was his responsibility and his fault, but John couldn't admit it and would never confess his opinion to Aston. He knew that he would make his father feel worse and that was the last thing he desired.

"It's exactly what I said. I let my selfishness win out and, now, look what I have done. I lost my wife while you and Sonya lost your mother forever and that's because of me," Aston said and leaned toward his son's shoulder.

"I think you should eat something and sleep." John was a strong man who had promised his mom to take care of his sister regardless of his personal cost. He had accepted the challenge but, pretty soon, he found himself trapped in the zone of lies and pretentiousness without being able to escape. But he would not lose his father too.

"Get some rest, Father."

John looked at his father and felt sorry for him. Aston was exhausted, his body cold. His hands were trembling and teardrops kept running down his pale cheeks.

"We can do this. Things will get better," his son whispered. He helped his father lay down and he grabbed the grey blanket from the chair. He covered his father's body and took off his shoes. He couldn't believe that his father was the one who needed support. His father's condition was driving him crazy; John suffocated as his soul carried on bleeding.

When Aston fell asleep, John walked toward the fireplace and knelt. Only the fire could see his face and the tears of his shattered heart. The flames of the fire, the snow and the freezing atmosphere would hide his weakness and keep his secret safe forever.

"I haven't thought seriously about something basic, John," his father murmured.

John was surprised since he thought his father was sleeping. Even so, he didn't turn around.

"What are you trying to say?" John was still gazing at the fire.

"Everything is in our minds. Our selfishness is the beginning of destruction," Aston confessed.

"I don't understand you," John answered.

"I thought I knew everything, but now I realize that I know nothing. I was selfish because I never trusted the opinions of the doctors. I never wanted to hear what they had to say about your mother's condition." His father couldn't stop crying. Aston felt the need to expose all the feelings he was hiding.

In contrast, John became angry and kept wondering about his father's stance. *How am I supposed to help him overcome all the difficulties?* John continued questioning himself as he stood up and left his father alone to sleep.

The dark had covered the whole place while the snowflakes carried on playing with the strong wind. John always liked looking up at the sky when it snowed. He loved staring at the snowflakes and, somehow, he believed he could see the path to heaven. The snowflakes served as the pure diamonds, the lights, which could help everyone, find his way to serenity.

The moment he got into the house again, his father was sitting on the sofa near to the fireplace. His eyes were captured by Erica's beauty and he kept holding tight her photograph as his thoughts were lost in the past. The memories must have been wonderful since Aston was smiling. He had shared many beautiful moments along with Erica as well.

"How are you?" John asked.

"I wish I could turn back the time." His father shook his head and then rolled his eyes.

"Unfortunately, this can't be done. But things will get better." John sat down next to him and caressed his father's back.

"How is this going to happen? Your sister doesn't even look at me." Aston was devastated. The tears appeared again and showed off his pale face and the deep wrinkles around his big eyes.

"Give her some time, things will change." John sounded angry and stood up.

"Think so?" Aston was obsessed with his daughter.

"Yes, Father," John said.

Aston looked around him and, out of the blue, he became nervous. He wanted to make sure there was no one else in the living room. His face had turned red while his silver hair carried on hiding his eyebrows. It was obvious that he wanted to share a secret with his son.

"I want you to promise me something," He whispered as his gaze locked on his son's eyes.

"What is it?" John asked.

"Your sister must never find out anything," Aston whispered.

"She could be in danger; I think we should tell her the truth." John sounded worried.

"Not now my son. She hates me and she would never accept the truth. She adored her mother." Aston would never ruin the best memories of his daughter.

"Yes, but is it safe? Can we actually do this?" John asked.

"We will do it. As long as I am alive, I will always be there for you and your sister." He smiled at his son while John nodded at him, although he had a different opinion.

Aston had ignored the emotional needs of his son many times during the past, but John had gotten used to his behavior.

"As you wish, Father." John had nothing else to add.

The cold night would keep their secret safe for many years.

During the following minutes, John and his father continued their serious discussion but, after a while, the depressive atmosphere changed. They recalled the funny moments and the times they were all sitting near the fireplace while playing, reading books, and listening to music.

The snow had covered the trees and the cars outside their house, while the dark secrets were locked in the cramped closets of their minds.

***

Sonya was still driving while the past continued flooding her thinking. There were so many memories, so many weird things and so many gaps, but she was eager to turn back the time to reveal the truth. She closed the window of her car and pulled her hair away from her face.

***

The sun's rays gave birth to optimism. It was a beautiful but cold day and Sonya was still in her bedroom. She was sitting in the red sofa looking outside the window. She liked the cold weather, the snow and she would never forget the times they were all playing outside the house.

The snowy days, her family used to run down the streets, yelling at one another while inviting their neighbors and everyone else to join their company.

"It was so beautiful," she whispered and hugged her favorite doll. That time, Sonya was fifteen and her dolls were her best friends.

The young girl gazed at her father who was talking on the phone while her brother was getting ready to go to work.

John put on his black coat and smiled at his sister. Sonya waved at him, ignoring her father, and remained distant without saying a word. There was a huge gap between them, but they had to find a solution to become a family again. They had to start talking.

"Sonya," Aston said.

"Yes." She stopped walking and waited to hear what her father had to say. His daughter was staring at the brown tile floor and didn't raise her eyes.

Aston squeezed his fingers and tried to stay calm. He took a deep breath and left the phone on the small desk while looking at his son.

"Come here, my child." Sonya moved closer, but was still somewhat defensive.

She needed to feel that she belonged somewhere; she wanted to become a part of her family again and she really missed hugs. Sonya was looking forward to sharing her thoughts and worries with the people she loved since there was no other way to heal the pain. She knew that without their support, she wouldn't survive.

"I'm listening, Father," she said.

The previous night Sonya couldn't sleep since she was thinking that she should be close to the rest of the members of her family to face up to their terrible experience. But she didn't know what to do, she felt like a stranger in her own house, and she couldn't explain why everything fought against her survival.

"Come closer," her father said.

"Okay." Sonya was ready to forgive Aston.

No matter what she thought he had done to her mother, she had to trust him and listen to him. She had decided to leave the nasty moments of the past behind and make a new beginning.

"How are you, my child?" Aston asked.

Her father stretched out his arms and offered his hands, but she remained where she was. Aston walked to her and she rushed to hide in his arms as the tears started running down her sweet face.

Her father felt her acceptance as the most precious gift he had ever received. He had never seen his daughter so vulnerable.

Then again, John liked seeing his father and his sister calm while, every minute that passed by, his admiration for his father's behavior started getting bigger and bigger since Aston was a special man.

John considered his father's presence in his life precious. Immediately, he replaced his worries about his job and the daily difficulties with thoughts of his father's patience and limitless love.

***

Since he was a small boy, Aston was his hero, the strongest man he had ever met and the best man on earth.

As far as his mother was concerned, John believed that she always liked overreacting and fighting for everything. Erica thought that Aston didn't love them, and of course she never stopped accusing him of anything in front of the kids. She used to imply that he was never there for their family, although she knew very well that her accusations were not true.

In reality, Erica was the one who had never really been there for her husband and for her kids. She didn't care about her family. She had never treated her children like a real mother; most times she seemed off somehow and drank. She used to say that everything had become too complicated for her. Sometimes she couldn't even take a step or change her clothes.

***

"How should I be, Father?" Sonya asked.

"We are here for you, my child. You have me and

52

your brother standing by your side, and we have you to help us become stronger. From now on, we will be the three of us, Sonya." Aston sounded calm.

The young girl hugged her father and didn't say anything else since all she had really missed was a kiss, a hug and a few nice words. But she also missed Erica, her mother, whose loss had made her absence intense.

For a moment, Erica's litanies flooded Sonya's thoughts. "Don't count on your father and don't count on men in general. They will betray you," Erica used to say to her daughter.

Sonya was about to leave her home since she believed her mother was right, but she was too young, she needed support, and they were never bad to her.

"I know that, Father," she murmured.

Sonya had decided to trust her father; she was not willing to behave like her mother. Sonya was able to see that Aston had never stopped trying to offer and provide his family with everything he could and, additionally, he was the one who had never forgotten her birthday. Despite his numerous trips all over the world, he had never missed the parties and the school contests.

"Everyone makes mistakes but you father is the exception to the rule, he is the champion. He knows how to screw things up," Erica loved saying to her kids.

Now it was like hearing her mother's voice trying to drown out Aston.

"Don't leave us out of your life, my child. Sonya, I am begging you to trust me because I need you, John needs you, and we don't want to lose you. Please forgive me for what I did to your mother." John looked angry but, on the other hand, he had promised some things to his father.

Sonya shook her head yes and squeezed her fingers on her father's black suit.

"We have to try this out," John said and, immediately, his black eyes pierced hers.

Sonya loved her brother so much that she would do everything for him. She would sacrifice her own happiness for him.

"I'm here. I love you," Sonya cried out.

Her brother smiled and, then, he looked at his father. They had made it; they were family again, even though John didn't like begging his sister to stay close to them. Although he was a successful cardiac surgeon like his father, he should have become an analyst to understand human nature. His father's plan confused him. Even so, he would never disappoint his father or betray his trust.

"We have to go back to work, but I want you to promise me that you will go back to school again," Aston said.

Sonya remained in her father's hug. She couldn't leave them, she had nowhere else to go and she would never survive out there alone. So she ignored her mother's sayings and followed her instincts. She had to comply with her needs and the needs of the rest of her family.

"I will go back to school. I just need a few more days to calm down," Sonya said.

"Okay."

For a couple of months, everything changed for the better, but it didn't last. Problems arose. And they fell apart again.

Chapter Five

"Everything will be fine. Things will get better." His mother leaned against the white door of his bedroom and glanced toward her son.

When she saw him disappointed, lying on the bed feeling lost, she waved her hands and, immediately, Ralph realized that his mother was trying to make him move on. She wanted to encourage him, but she couldn't find the most appropriate words to say in order to help him cheer up.

"Think so?" he asked vaguely.

"I am sure Sonya will come back," she answered and the pained smile reappeared on her sweet face.

That moment Ralph felt lucky--he was relieved and he realized that his mother's presence was precious. Every time she looked at him, it was obvious that she would never abandon her son. His gaze was seeking for sympathy. Ralph was sure that he could do nothing without her support.

The daylight wasn't sufficient enough to do everything; he had to be at work, to take care of his baby and to search for his wife. Mrs. Pears was everything Ralph needed and he would never forget his mother's help.

"Why did she leave?" he asked.

"I have no idea. But I am sure that she never stopped loving you." His mother's opinion managed to heal the pain in his soul. At least he had someone to be there for him and his mother stood by their side without saying anything negative about Sonya. She had never made complaints about her personality.

"Did you do anything wrong?" Mrs. Pears asked.

"No, Mother, I did nothing wrong," Ralph answered testily.

He got up from the bed and avoided looking his

mother in the eye. As much as Ralph was trying to hide his true feelings, he was very angry and his mother could clearly see that.

"Don't get angry," she said as she took a few steps and stood behind her son.

"I'm fine, Mom."

He was furious since the disappointment along with the anger had enveloped his thoughts, and he could do nothing to change his mood. He kept shaking and he fought against everything while, at the same time, he had to abstain from thinking about her.

Ralph had to forget the beautiful moments they had shared in the past. His true desire was to hate his partner, focus on his child's happiness and move on his life.

"Did you call her family?" His mother asked while he was still looking outside the big window of the white bedroom.

What was he supposed to tell her? Sonya had never talked to him about her family, he knew nothing about her family.

"No," he mumbled and turned back while, soon, his eyes pierced hers.

"Does she have a family?" His mother wouldn't stop asking questions. Mrs. Pears was waiting for an answer, and she was patient enough to hear something, but Ralph had nothing to say.

She placed her hands on her son's face and smiled at him.

How was he supposed to tell her that he didn't know anything about her family?

"Yes, I guess she has a family," Ralph whispered as he felt guilty. His mind traveled back to the time when he had confessed his feelings to Sonya.

Love at first sight. Everyone knew about it, no one could fight the romantic affection of the moonlight in his heart.

Suddenly, Ralph realized that he had screwed things up and could do nothing to change his life. He was twenty-one years old, his partner was missing, his baby was sleeping, his mother was taking care of him and his daughter and, furthermore, he had to keep his work to raise his child and to maintain his independence. The dreams and the plans he had had about his studies and becoming an analyst had turned into ash.

Ralph had rushed to do everything on his own, while his family had warned him about the obstacles he would come across. They wanted to protect him, but they would never impose their decisions and opinions on him. Ralph was free to live his life the way he wanted and he just did it. He thought it was going to be easy, but Ralph was wrong. If only he knew…

On the other hand, he could never imagine that he would be alone. Betrayal was one of the words he hated and it had never crossed his mind since Sonya had found the way to earn his trust and make him believe in their relationship in no time.

"Why don't you call them?" his mother suggested and sounded anxious as she took a deep breath and tried to hide her curiosity since she respected her son's agony.

Mrs. Pears pulled her long, black hair back and smiled at her son again. She was there to support Ralph; she didn't like shooting her son with difficult and unfair questions. She adored Ralph, she would never judge him.

"I know nothing about her family," he said.

His mother rolled her eyes and sat down on the bed. Ralph sat down next to her and waited for a suggestion.

Sonya always avoided telling him things concerning her parents, her family and her experiences from Chicago. She had never talked to him about her family and, surprisingly, Ralph had accepted her stance; he had respected her privacy because he was sure that when she would be ready, Sonya would talk to him about everything.

His mother's silence and the way she gazed at him reminded him of the first time he had asked Sonya about her parents. She started crying, making him feel like the worst person on earth.

"I see," his mother whispered.

Now, Ralph was able to understand the reasons his parents were against his decision to get married and start his own family.

Ralph and Sonya didn't know one another well; in truth, Ralph knew nothing about Sonya's family. He believed that the enthusiasm, the good chemistry and the good sex would be enough to keep them together forever.

How could I be so stupid? Ralph wondered. He wanted to get away to find himself again and remake the rules which would help him find his way to the path of a happy life.

"I have to see the baby." He heard the baby crying and stood up since he needed to escape.

Ralph wasn't prepared to face up his mother and to deal seriously with reality. He couldn't accept the fact that life and Sonya had treated him badly. He thought he was naïve and he couldn't overcome this feeling.

"I will do that. You need to sleep," his mother said and got up.

His mother left him alone, not wanting to seem weak. Mrs. Pears was a strong woman who believed in romance and love at first sight. She was sure that things would get better, she was aware of the destination of true love, but she had no idea about the journey. At least, she was positive.

"Thanks," Ralph whispered and lay down.

"You're welcome, honey," his mother said and went into the baby's room.

Ralph closed his eyes and, before long, he fell asleep. He was exhausted; he didn't have the energy to take off his shoes and his clothes. In a few hours, the nasty experience had changed everything. Ralph looked different and didn't have the mood and the strength to deal with anything.

On the other hand, the weird dreams continued destroying him since he couldn't escape and felt like he was living the same story again and again. His meeting with Sonya and the way their relationship evolved had haunted his mind and Ralph couldn't get away.

***

In less than a week, they had become one. They were having fun and they loved walking down the streets meeting new people, new places, kissing one another, remaining crazy in love. They adored strolling around the famous avenues and dazzling the amazing New York hand in hand, and sharing loving looks. They had the chance to do everything they desired and dreamed of. It was great living in the center of the world and doing the things you like with your special partner.

In time, Ralph and Sonya decided to live together, and about a month after their first meeting, Sonya moved to his apartment and he was thrilled. Everything was great; he was glad and crazy in love with his girlfriend, looking forward to doing everything with her for the rest of their lives.

"I haven't done anything yet," Sonya confessed and blushed. She was anxious, and looked into his eyes. "Would you like me to make love to you?" Ralph asked and placed his forehead on hers, waiting patiently for her answer.

"Yes," Sonya whispered and kissed his lips.

The first night they spent together was wonderful and unique. Sonya's nervousness dissipated completely when she felt his naked body next to her. She loved touching Ralph and she loved feeling his hands on her skin. When he hugged her tight and started spreading his kisses all over her body, Sonya surrendered and, immediately, they both felt the engagement of their souls. That moment they were both sure they were meant to be together.

***

As time passed by, they carried on dealing with their studies and their happiness since they had an amazing relationship and an incredible chemistry. They looked like a married couple and no one could deny that.

They were still not sure about what they would do in the future, but they didn't stop discovering their selves. They were both in their early twenties and were also aware of their likes and of all those they wanted to avoid. Ralph was not eager to spend the rest of his life doing something he didn't like, and neither was Sonya.

Before long, they both found jobs and tried to become independent because Ralph hated spending his family's money and Sonya hated exploiting her father's wealth. Although they never lacked anything, they needed to feel strong by making their own money, depending exclusively on their abilities.

"What are we going to do?" Sonya sounded.

"I want to become a doctor," Ralph said and Sonya leaned on his chest.

"Really...?" she asked vaguely.

"I want to become an analyst." He sounded confident about his decision. Sonya shook her head and smiled at him while she seemed proud of him.

"That's great, honey," she answered and caressed his naked skin.

"What would you like to do?" Ralph was curious about her plans. He would do everything to help her achieve her goals.

"I would like to become an architect," Sonya confessed as Ralph was taken aback.

"Why are we wasting our time? Why do we keep doing things we don't like?" Ralph wondered.

"I have no idea, my lovely analyst," Sonya bit her

lips and laughed.

Then, they started teasing one another and made love again. They kept talking and analyzing anything until they fell asleep. Ralph was very tired since he had to work as a barman and to study as well, but he was happy because he really loved his new way of life; he had a home and a lovely girlfriend.

The following day Ralph woke up earlier than usual and Sonya wasn't next to him. He started calling out for her, but he got no answer. Soon, he discovered that she was sitting on the bench in the balcony, gazing at the park and the skyscrapers.

Sonya loved the view and she liked drinking her coffee here while making the plans for the rest of the day. Ralph took a few more steps and invaded her world, bringing her back to life and reality.

"Who is Erica?" Ralph asked and raised the cup of the coffee toward his lips.

"What?" Sonya was taken aback; she started wondering about the things he knew.

"Who is Erica?" Ralph sounded

"My mother!" Sonya answered angrily, flushing. "Why?"

"Last night you didn't stop calling out for her," Ralph said, startled by her reaction His gaze focused on her eyes but he didn't smile at her.

"What?" Now, she pulled her long hair away from her face and fixed her eyes on him. A torrent of tears made obvious her feelings.

On the other hand, Ralph could tell that she was surprised; he couldn't explain her facial expression. She looked angry, sad, and panicked, all at the same time.

Ralph left the cup of the coffee on the wooden table and went next to her where he knelt and later caressed her back. When his eyes locked on hers, he felt that he had to do something.

Then again, Sonya felt awful since she was still trying to hide the truth. Ralph pulled her hair away from her pale face again and decided to speak up.

"You've never talked to me about your family," he whispered, hoping she would say something.

"They are dead, I have no one," Sonya said without hesitation.

Ralph took Sonya in his arms and held her tight.-He felt like a jerk. Sonya leaned on his chest. The tears kept running down her face and she remained silent, avoiding adding anything more.

"What happened?" Ralph asked.

"Car accident…" Sonya whispered and hid her head in his hug.

"How old were you?" Ralph asked again.

"I was five," she murmured.

"I'm sorry, baby," he locked her in his hug and stopped asking questions.

"Listen, Ralph, I don't want to talk about it, I'm not ready yet." Sonya abstained from looking at him.

"Okay, baby, I respect that," he said.

Ralph would never let her go.

***

Suddenly, Ralph woke up and screamed her name. Sweat was running down his face and had already soaked the pillows. He sat up, took a deep breath, and turned the pillows over. *Try to sleep*, he thought. But, unfortunately, the same dream insisted on killing all of his hopes.

***

They counted a year since their first meeting. They both loved sharing their lives as a real couple. Every time they walked toward their apartment building, the noisy neighborhood used to pay attention to them. The beautiful ladies from the colorful shops and their neighbors liked talking and shaking hands with the beautiful couple.

Then again, their friends didn't stop laughing at

them; everyone believed they were acting unusual; they used to call them romantic freaks. Every Friday they loved spending their nights at their favorite bar talking about everything. They were all young and looked forward to discovering the paths the future held for them. Ralph and Sonya were the exception to the rule since they had found whatever they looked for.

All of them kept teasing the young couple, but in truth, they were all jealous of Ralph and Sonya since they had managed to build and sustain a beautiful relationship.

"You are almost twenty-one years old! Don't you want to meet and have sex and fun with other people?" they used to tell them, but every time, Ralph and Sonya ignored their suggestions.

During the first year of their relationship, everything had changed. They were living together and carried on making dreams and plans for the future since they were the happiest people on earth. They were young, healthy and independent, and they never stopped hoping that things between them would always remain perfect. They loved having realistic aspirations and they never gave up on trying achieving their goals.

Living together was interesting for both of them because they had to follow each other's rules. Sonya hated seeing Ralph's clothes on the sofa while Ralph felt weird when he had to clean his things and help Sonya with housekeeping as well. The first weeks, nervousness and curiosity had taken over but, later, funny grimaces and jokes accompanied these tasks.

As far as their professional futures were concerned, they had both made up their minds. They were sure about what they wanted to do; Sonya was studying architecture while Ralph had decided to become an analyst and nothing would make him change his plans.

***

"What are you thinking?" he asked.

"Nothing," she whispered, but something about her reply made him worry.

Sonya placed her head on his chest and rested her hands on his legs as he smelled her blonde hair, thinking of their future. Ralph began caressing her back and he was able to feel her heartbeat. His partner was nervous, but was not willing to speak up yet.

Although Sonya looked calm, she wasn't as peaceful as usual. They were lying on the grass under the large pine trees, gazing at the students passing by, but there was something strange flying in the air, turning the cold weather even colder, causing uncertainty for both of them. The mystery had started spreading through the air and the doubt began rising, confusing Ralph's mind.

"What do you think about us?" Sonya asked.

"What do you mean?" he sounded serious while he continued playing with her hair.

At first, Ralph was taken aback because over the last few days Sonya seemed distant and, additionally, there were some moments where he wanted to hold her in his arms, and she avoided coming closer to him. There was something going on and he was definitely sure about that. The previous night Ralph wanted to have sex with Sonya, but when he touched her body, she stepped back and didn't have the least of intention of feeling his body on hers.

"How do you imagine your life in future, let's say in five years?" she asked.

"I don't know." Ralph smiled since he had no serious answer, and because they were only twenty-one years old.

How are we supposed to make plans for the future when we are still in the process of growing up, working on our inner feelings and learning to comply with our insecurities? he considered silently.

"Do you think we could still be together?" she asked again.

"I love you; you love me, so yeah, why shouldn't we be together?" he was confused, he had no idea what she was trying to say.

"Do you really love me?" Sonya sounded anxious and didn't look at him.

"Yes, Sonya, I love you very much." He meant every single word he told her.

Sonya moved up her head and hugged him as he placed his hands on her back and felt her crazy heartbeat again. He couldn't explain her reaction. She looked scared and her pale complexion gave birth to pessimism.

"I have to tell you something." She looked extremely anxious—her facial expression made him worry.

Sonya looked up at the sky.

"What is it, baby? Are you okay?" he asked, as the love of his life began shaking.

Sonya ignored his question; she didn't even look at him, and that moment he froze in fear, Ralph began feeling weird. He believed she wanted to break up with him.

"What is it, baby?" Ralph asked again as he prayed to God not to let this happen.

Sonya caught her breath and placed her hands on his cheeks.

"I'm pregnant," Sonya whispered as tears started running down her face.

"What…?" He panicked.

"I have a baby in my belly," she murmured.

Sonya was looking forward to seeing his first reaction. Her big, blue eyes were locked on his as he was trying to recover from her confession and pull himself back together. It was the most unexpected announcement in his entire life.

"Do you want this child?" she asked.

"Yes, of course I want this baby," he answered impulsively.

Actually, he had no time to think anything other

than the safety of his lovely partner, and he would never let her down. Ralph was pretty sure that Sonya was the special girl he was seeking for since he was seventeen and she was the best woman to become the mother of his child.

On the other hand, Ralph was not aware of his responsibility yet; he knew nothing concerning the raising of a child, but he thought he would make it. Sonya's presence was the strangest, the most unexpected and the most beautiful experience in his life, but now, he was face-to-face with the most critical moment of his living and his decision would affect his and Sonya's future forever.

"Are you sure?" Sonya gazed at him and smiled.

"Yes, Sonya. Do you want this child?" he asked.

"Yes," she said with a little laugh and, immediately, he hugged her and didn't stop kissing her, stealing everyone's attention.

Ralph and Sonya had two options, and they chose to become parents. They were two kids who had decided to accept the challenge, ignoring the difference between reality and theory. Although they were determined to test the waters and dared to move on the next level of their relationship and life, they had no idea what they would come across.

Sometimes you have to risk, and being twenty-one years old means that you have the nerves to act immediately. But you might behave instinctively and maybe wrong as well, Ralph thought and found himself trapped in a critical dilemma.

Ralph and Sonya never regretted for keeping their baby because they truly loved one another and they both felt that this was enough. As expected, they neglected their studies and focused on their new responsibilities, postponing their plans and their dreams. They were surrounded by the cloud of euphoria and they kept enjoying their walks, hand in hand, fully in love, optimistic and ready to welcome the new member of their union in their life. They were impatient to see the sweetest face of all.

***

Ralph heard his baby crying and got up, but he heard his mother who had already run into Shania's room, singing and whispering to his daughter.

This is insane, he thought. *Sonya should have been here. She didn't have to abandon us and it was not supposed to be this way.*

He went back in his bed, and the moment Ralph covered his body with the cold sheets, he felt like there were silver blades on his skin, ready to hurt and kill his soul. He was still thinking of Sonya.

Chapter Six

"hat is it this time?" Sonya wondered as she put the baby on the small pink bed and rushed to answer the phone call.

As usual, Sonya was in panic. She looked different and didn't stop running like a maniac, taking care of her baby who kept seeking for her attention and cleaning the house as well. Meanwhile, it was obvious that the pregnancy had stolen her energy and had changed her shape since Sonya had lost her glow, her smile and her carefree mood while she fought very hard to get her tight and beautiful body back. She always hated being fat, she would never forget her childhood when the boys used to call her fatty Sonya.

The phone rang again as she was trying to find the pink blanket to cover up her daughter.

"Who is it?" she asked angrily, picking up.

"Sonya?"

The moment she heard his voice, she was taken aback since she realized that she actually hadn't managed to get away.

Sonya pulled her messy, blonde hair away from her pale face and continued dealing with her baby. She took her daughter in her arms and, then, she headed toward the window of the baby's room.

"Yes," she said.

"How are you?"

"I'm fine," Sonya said and tried to sound cool.

"I was trying to reach you." She would never forget her brother's voice.

"Why is that?" Sonya asked.

"I would like to see you," John said.

Sonya half-closed her eyes and placed her forehead on the cold window. Her daughter stretched out her tiny arms and tried to caress her mother's face, trying to make her feel happy, while Sonya smiled and kissed her beautiful hands. If only she could delete the nasty past and the ugly moments from her memory forever.

"I'm afraid that's not possible. I'm busy." Sonya gazed at her baby and smiled at her.

"Yes, I know that. You found a nice guy and, now, you are a mom," he said, and as always John had the ability to surprise people.

"How do you know?" Sonya asked.

"I know everything," he said, making Sonya nervous.

"What do you want?" Sonya asked again.

"I want to see you."

"Why do you want to see me?" Sonya sounded curious and impatient.

"You missed me."

The moment Sonya heard him laughing, she closed the phone and threw it down on a chair. She took a deep breath and started walking around in the baby's room watching her daughter who had already fallen asleep in her embrace.

"I love you so much," she whispered and gave her baby another kiss on her head.

"I don't believe it," Sonya murmured.

When she heard the doorbell, she felt the need to protect her baby. She put her daughter in her bed and closed the door of Shania's room behind her, then walked hurriedly toward the stairs. She had no idea what to do. *What does he want?* she questioned herself. *More lies?*

"I'm coming!"

Sonya stood in front of the mirror and tried to tidy herself up. She hated seeing people feeling sorry for the changes the pregnancy had caused to her body and style. Sonya didn't like her hair, her pale skin, her dry lips and the black circles under her eyes. She didn't like her clothes either; she hated being fat and the red pants and the yellow jacket she was wearing made her look awful.

"How am I going to fix this mess?" she used to say since she came back home from the hospital with her baby.

Sonya was suffering from depression and didn't have the positive energy she needed to deal with the new phase she was going through. She lacked emotional stability and felt that she couldn't rely on Ralph since most times he was coming home late.

On the other hand, Ralph was having a hard time too; he had to do everything properly while struggling to adjust to reality. Either he would be at work or at school, striving to do anything. He worried about his partner and their baby, and he always wanted to make sure they missed nothing.

The doorbell sounded like grenade exploding in her mind and, unfortunately, there was no one there to calm her down since Ralph had to be at work.

"Wait a second!" When Sonya opened the door, she became furious. She didn't smile and she wasn't polite.

"Hi, Sonya, how are you?" John sounded confident.

"What do you want, John?" Sonya asked.

"Might I come in?" Sonya let him come into her house and closed the door.

They walked into the living room and sat down. The secrets of the past were going to be revealed, the promises would be broken, and Sonya and Ralph's nightmare would begin.

Chapter Seven

R alph could still remember the first day they went to the stores to look for clothes for their baby. It was one of the best days in his life.

The moment they stepped into the babies' department, he felt euphoria running in his veins and couldn't stop smiling. Ralph looked at Sonya and took a deep breath while he couldn't stop pointing at the tiny clothes, smelling the wonderful scent and enjoying every single moment with the mother of his child.

When Ralph glanced at Sonya he recalled the first time he saw his partner, when he felt adrenalin running in his veins. He was hesitant but he fought against his fears and, finally, he earned her trust and her love.

Fifteen months after their first meeting, he was able to realize that both his lovely lady and his daughter had managed to affect his living and make him dream of beautiful scenes since his spirit and existence were solid connected with the air they breathed. Ralph's life was based on their presences and he was thrilled. Sonya and his daughter had managed to mark every single cell of his mind.

"I want to buy everything!" Sonya said as Ralph nodded at her and laughed.

It was definitely the most incredible experience he had ever come across. The smell of the tiny clothes was amazing, and that moment, he looked forward to holding his baby in his arms.

The previous night, he seemed weird—since Dr. Jamson told them the sex of the baby--but, soon, Ralph came back to reality and found his great mood again. When they stepped out of the doctor's office, he was disappointed. He had been impatient to hear that they would welcome a boy in their home, but he got over it immediately since Sonya woke him up.

"The second will be a boy," she told him to reassure him that he would have the chance to watch the football games with his boy and admire his son as an excellent athlete too.

The following seven months Ralph and Sonya used to spend their weekends searching and buying clothes, games, posters and everything else they could imagine for their baby, and they were both extremely excited. Every night was the same with the previous one; they walked hand in hand, Sonya was eating ice cream while Ralph used to hold the bags with the things they had bought for the lucky baby.

It was the best period of their life; Sonya was thrilled and loved spending hours in bed reading books about pregnancy and babies. She had learned almost everything and she had never missed to ask questions to the doctor about the way she should feed and wash their baby.

"Take it easy, Sonya. You will make it," Dr. Jamson used to tell her to calm her.

Then again, Ralph had to work very hard to maintain their financial stability while during his free time he loved going out with Sonya and their friends talking about the future, the name of the baby and the activities their daughter should attend.

It is so beautiful sharing my life with Sonya, Ralph used to think.

***

Unfortunately, after Sonya's unanticipated reaction, Ralph was certain he would never be able to get this experience out of his mind since she had done the worst thing. She had betrayed him; Sonya had murdered his trust and his pure feelings.

It was the second night his partner was not home and Ralph could do nothing other but keep thinking of the very first moments of his worst nightmare.

***

When Ralph finished his work, he went back home to share his joy with his family. He was still working as a bartender, and as usual, he was in high spirits since he had become a father-- the best achievement in his entire life. When he first saw his daughter's beautiful eyes, he fell for her immediately.

Sonya had quit her job (actually, she never liked dealing with sales), while Ralph continued struggling to earn their independency, making his own money to raise his child and offer his partner whatever she needed.

That day as usual, Ralph had bought candies and ice cream—it was his way to thank his partner and make obvious his appreciation for everything she had done for him. Sonya loved ice cream and she adored all the flavors, but white chocolate was her favorite.

While driving back home, Ralph couldn't get them out of his mind; he squeezed his long fingers on the wheel of his car and rushed to get home. He was looking forward to holding his baby and his partner in his arms, and he didn't stop singing his favorite songs since he was delighted and he could sense euphoria, optimism and the absolute happiness flooding his body, his heart and his spirit.

The moment Ralph saw his home, he parked, and watched to them. After a while, he got out of the black BMW while, at the same time, the snowflakes were doing their beautiful magic tricks.

The snow had already covered everything an inch deep. He was sure that the upcoming storm would make things more difficult and would make them feel trapped in their home. But he didn't really care since his partner and his baby would be safe and they would have plenty of time to play, sing, read tales and laugh at one another. Besides, Sonya and Shania waited patiently for Ralph, and his partner also loved knowing that she had a strong man to protect both of them. Sonya was sure that Ralph would sacrifice his life for her and for Shania.

January 7, the winter and the strong wind along with the snow had turned the state into a cold but wonderful paradise as well. Their new place seemed amazing. Ralph looked around him and gazed upon the sky of their small, quite neighborhood.

Ralph and Sonya had decided to leave New York since they regarded that Long Island was the best area to raise their children and, for the time being, they thought they were right. For the last three months they had the privilege to wake up and stare at the pine trees, the large roofs and the less noisy roads. They had managed to change their life entirely and they were really, really happy.

Without any further delay, Ralph put his black hat on his head and wore his black gloves remembering the time Sonya had bought them for him; it was during the first week they dated. She knew he loved winter and she wanted to protect him from the cold days and the snow.

Ralph rubbed his eyes and smiled. He was crazy in love and he never doubted about Sonya's honest behavior because his partner had always made obvious her feelings to him and she never hesitated to show her love.

Before long, Ralph walked slowly toward the white front door of their home, and he could bet that he heard their baby crying, like asking for help and attention.

Ralph shook his head and thought of his beautiful partner. He knew very well that Sonya was exhausted and he could clearly see that the pregnancy and the constant needs of their daughter had stolen her power. Sonya lacked of time to deal with herself, to take care of her health, to rest, to eat well and have some sleep. Her eyes were always swollen and she was worried about her body since she looked forward to getting her figure back.

Now, Ralph was sure that he heard their baby crying, and wondered about his partner. Sonya adored their baby and he was pretty sure that she would make it.

When Ralph closed the white front door of their home behind him, he sensed there was something terrible going on, and he couldn't explain that weird feeling. He was able to feel the negative energy.

The moment he started calling out her name, he felt lost in a frozen wasteland. His lovely partner never showed up. Ralph could still hear his baby crying but there was no sign of Sonya.

Ralph panicked. He went upstairs and ran into their daughter's room. He took Shania in his arms and, at the same time, Shania stopped crying.

Ralph would never forget the way his daughter looked at him the moment he stretched out his arms and locked her in his hug. She was safe with him.

Later, Ralph took off his hat and his black coat while his daughter was staring at him, caressing his cheeks and making strange sounds. He began searching the whole house to find Sonya.

Out of the blue, Shania started laughing and he felt wonderful. *At least she is happy,* he thought and smiled at Shania who looked like an angel.

Ralph looked for his partner everywhere, but Sonya was gone and he didn't understand why. She hadn't left a note, a message or something else to let him know what had happened. She had just vanished.

Ralph sat down on the brown sofa in their living room and waited for his partner, while his daughter was sleeping peacefully in his arms, breathing the air of relief.

Ralph was helpless, he worried about his partner and he couldn't stop wondering about her behavior. She had never done something like that before and he couldn't believe that she had acted this way.

The weather conditions had changed; the low temperatures kept increasing the danger of being hurt, and the strong wind could cause problems to those who were out there, away from their houses.

Ralph half-closed his eyes and shook his head, feeling grateful to God for seeing his daughter safe and healthy. But where was Sonya?

Chapter Eight

"Aston is dead," John said as he took off his black leather jacket and stood in front of the beautiful painting of his sister's baby.

When John looked back, Sonya remained still. She looked as cold and lifeless as a statue.

"What...what happened?" she asked.

"Heart attack, he didn't suffer," John said softly. Sonya sank in the brown chair and put her head in her hands.

"Are you sorry?" her brother asked.

"Off course I am!" Sonya's eyes latched angrily on his.

"Don't be. Besides, you hated him. Just to know, he was the one who should have hated you." John sounded impatient, abrasive.

Sonya shook her head.

"I don't understand. What are you trying to say?" she asked.

"I would like a drink." John was confident; he would never find it difficult having a discussion where he would still command the impressions and the attention, becoming the winner.

"I have nothing for you," his sister said as John smiled and didn't insist.

"I am your brother," he said.

"Just save it." Sonya wanted to get rid of him; there was no love between them anymore. She would never forget the second day she had come to New York.

***

Sonya had called her brother and, by accident, she had heard his conversation with his girlfriend. "I hate Sonya. She is a bitch. I never want to see her again. I hope she dies," he'd said as he hung up.

***

"I like your house," he said now.

John looked curious about her life since her current living had nothing to do with the way she had been raised. He could see a small house with a cramped living room and a tiny kitchen, which couldn't be compared with the mansion they had grown up.

"Bitches have houses too," she said and gazed at her brother. She could feel the sweat in her hands; she wanted to slap him.

"That hurt, but it was good," he said.

"Say what you want and get out of my house." "Unfortunately, my father screwed up everything and, now, you will get two million dollars. I will get the same money as you, and I believe this is unfair. I wanted to make sure that you knew the truth, which is why I am here, talking with you." John knelt in front of his sister, unsmiling.

"I'm sure you meant *our* father," Sonya said.

"No, honey, I said *my* father." John bit his lips.

"Are you drunk?" Sonya gazed at him.

"No, Sonya, I am not drunk." He got up.

"What are you saying?" She stood up and waited. John turned back and looked into her eyes.

"Our mother was a crazy bitch. When I was nine, she left our house and didn't say anything to me or my father. For a while we believed she was dead, but a year later she came back. Erica came back pregnant and I guess you can understand that Aston was not your biological father. But he forgave our mother, and adopted you." John seemed to enjoy their conversation. After all, he waited for too long to reveal the truth and hurt his sister for her behavior and the way she'd always dealt with his father.

"I don't believe you." John grabbed his jacket and revealed an envelope and placed it into his sister's hands. Sonya sat down in the chair whereas her brother turned back again and gazed at the painting of the baby.

"Might I see my niece? In spite of everything, we

are still siblings," John said with a little laugh. Shania looked like her mother and John was able to remember Sonya's first moments into their home.

"Get out of my house." Sonya got up and left the envelope on the small table. She pushed her brother away and started punching him. Out of the blue, Sonya started screaming and, in no time, she kicked him out of her house.

"I bet your father is a crazy, stupid creep like you. My father was the best of all and you never appreciated what he did for you."

"Go to hell." Sonya slammed the door in his face and locked it.

She ran to the living room, and grabbed the envelope. She wanted to know everything.

"Oh my God…" she murmured.

It was time to go.

Chapter Nine

"I don't want to leave you alone," Mrs. Pears said and loosened her shoulders.

"Why is that?" Ralph asked.

"I want to stay with you. Besides, you still need me."

When his mother looked at him, Ralph couldn't offer a word. His mother was right; he needed help, and mostly, he needed someone to take care of his baby. It was Sunday morning, his favorite day.

***

Ralph and Sonya loved spending Sunday mornings in bed doing nothing else than making love, reading newspapers and eating ice-ream and chocolates. They loved that day of the week; the young couple adored doing simple, silly things to get away from the routine of the weekdays.

***

The next moment Ralph knelt and stood in front of the sofa, gazing at his precious treasure, his baby. He smiled at his daughter and took her in his arms as she didn't stop stretching out her arms and shaking her tiny fingers to make her father act.

"Let's have a walk," Ralph suggested and gazed upon his mother.

Mrs. Pears nodded at him and then they ran toward the car, getting past his serious problems for a while. Ralph was acting like a teenager again and, fortunately, his mother stood by his side and never stopped supporting him. Every time she looked at him, she had the ability to change his thinking and make him focus on his baby.

Whenever Ralph felt the need to get away, Mrs Pears was the one who reminded him of his responsibility. And he would do everything in order to see his daughter laughing and waving her tiny hands at him.

***

For the last two days, they both had to be very patient without losing their hopes. During the nights, Ralph used to stay in bed struggling to forget Sonya's betrayal by fighting back tears, while his mother, after checking out and seeing that her granddaughter was asleep, used to sink in the sofa downstairs thinking of Sonya, hoping that if she did come home, that she and Ralph and Shania could remake their lives together.

Although Mrs. Pears didn't know her well, she would never forget the first time she met her son's partner. Yes, in her view Sonya was very beautiful and she truly loved her son. Every time Sonya gazed at Ralph, Mrs. Pears could see the reflection of love into her big blue eyes.

As far as Ralph was concerned, he would never get used to her absence because, somehow, Sonya had managed to haunt his mind and trap his soul in her world. Ralph was living a tragedy; he was looking forward to giving an end to this freaking nightmare. A tornado of emotions had swept through him, forcing him from reality.

Ralph would never overcome her betrayal and keep on having fun, sharing carefree moments with others since he always loved doing everything with Sonya. Every minute that passed by, he was trying to figure out the reason she had left their home and their baby. Ralph kept asking questions to himself but, as usual, he ran into failure after failure because he was sure they had no serious problems. In truth, there was never any serious misunderstanding between them and they had never stopped compromising.

Ralph was angry with the mother of his child because he thought that Sonya ought to talk to him first about her feelings and her future plans. Instead, his partner had never said anything to him about the pressure she obviously felt, and he would never forgive her for the way she reacted. If only she had opened her heart…

Then again, Sonya didn't make any effort to contact him, and that made Ralph wonder about his role, his stance and the importance of his presence in her life while being together and having a beautiful relationship covered by the veil of love and harmony.

Either Ralph had become a boring partner or Sonya needed something different, a wind of change that would give her the energy she was missing to move on. Ralph could explain nothing as he continued running into despair since he always believed that Sonya was really happy with him. It seemed that Ralph was living in his microcosm, in his ideal world where everything was perfect. He was happy whereas he assumed that Sonya was not.

As far as her unbelievable behavior and reaction toward the baby was concerned, Ralph remained angry with his partner because of the way she had treated their daughter. Sonya had no right to ignore, neglect and abandon their child. Shania was her child, Sonya was the one who had given birth to that sweet, little creature and, additionally, she really wanted to keep their baby. Sonya was against abortions; if she had proceeded to that crime, she would never forgive herself. And Ralph was pretty sure that she would give her life for their little girl.

The last night, Ralph realized that the moment Sonya erased the past and decided to live her life without them, she must have forgotten everything.

***

"I want some hot chocolate," Mrs. Pears said.

Ralph stared at his mother and felt grateful to God for sending her to help him out with the mess, which dominated in his life. For once more, she smiled at him, sharing her optimism and energy with her son.

Ralph half-closed his eyes, he wasn't still sure if he would make it without her support. Along with Shania, currently, they were the only people who had managed to make him hope that things would get better, and that miracles do happen every day.

"Okay," he said, and after bundling Shania up, they headed toward the nearby small café. He smiled and seemed happy. He'd really needed that walk.

During their stroll, Ralph's mother kept pointing at the beautiful, white cedar-trees, which surrounded the white grass in an effort to make her son forget his worries and devastating thoughts, which wanted to tear apart his mood.

***

Mrs. Pears always loved gardening, she loved the trees, and since Ralph was a kid, he always remembered his mother dealing with her countless flowers and her lovely roses. He had seen many times her long, black hair dusty, but she had never complained about the time and the energy she used to spend to take care of them.

***

The scene was wonderful; the picture they kept watching made them smile and breathe the air of emancipation. The beauty of the white park remained amazing since the benches, the stone paths and the lakes, which were covered by the snow, looked awesome. The snowflakes had done a great job and everyone carried on admiring the beauty of the cold nature. It would have been lovely, if only Sonya was there.

Mother and son continued enjoying their carefree walk, and as it seemed, Ralph had changed his mood and looked different since he didn't stop smiling. He really needed this walk to get away from the dark thoughts, which were thirsty to envelope, his spirit, his optimism and his instincts forever.

"Honey, look over there!" his mother exclaimed while she pointed across from them at something unexpected.

Ralph froze. There she was, in plain view. Sonya.

She was standing by a bench, chatting to several

cats.

His first thought was for his daughter, for her future and happiness. He was afraid that Shania would never see her mother as she was used to be again, and she would always ask him questions about her life and the reasons she had left home and had dumped them.

For the last two days Ralph had abstained from telling his mother what he was thinking because he hoped that Sonya would come back home, but every second that passed by, the chances of returning back carried on drowning in the ocean of vanity.

Ralph counted more than forty-eight hours after the moment his partner closed the door of their house behind her and never came back, and he had decided to stop asking questions about her unanticipated move. If she didn't like wasting her time with Ralph anymore, he would accept it. But he needed a clear and honest answer as well.

Soon, police would start searching for Sonya, although the detectives had informed him that there were not many possibilities to find her immediately. The police officers were sure that Sonya had left home; they had told Ralph they had seen the same scenario many times, but they didn't miss to reassure him that his partner was not in danger. They had checked out the whole house and the quite neighborhood for more than three hours. "We can do nothing yet. We have to wait. Try to be patient. It happens often." Ralph hated their official answer, he hated those four sentences, but the police officers were right.

Ralph felt the need to scream and expose his anger and disappointment by breaking everything he could see, but he was sure that he wouldn't bring her back because it was her decision. Besides, he was against violence and nasty behavior in the house and he would never do something that would make his daughter and his mother upset.

On the other hand, Mrs. Pears believed that Sonya

needed some time to adjust to reality and remake the rules of her new role. Sonya was not just a young lady anymore; she was a young mother, an aspiring young lady who had many dreams and aspirations. She regarded that her son's partner had to be away from their home for a while to pull herself back together. Mrs. Pears was still certain that Sonya would never leave their home for good because she really cared about her daughter and partner, and the middle-aged woman always trusted her instincts.

"Everything will be fine," his mother said now.

Ralph had made up his mind. Sonya's reaction was unacceptable, but he needed to hear some straight answers. He would do his best to delete her existence and her presence from his life.

"Things will change," Mrs. Pears reassured him, trying to calm him.

"Actually, I don't care." he said. He was angry— but he was also in love.

His mother smiled again and placed her left hand around his waist as he kept holding his daughter tight in his arms while having her tiny palms in his hand.

"What's wrong with Sonya? Have you done anything bad to her?" his mother asked.

Ralph remained steady on the grey, stone path while Shania kept squeezing his hands. It was her favorite habit; she liked squeezing everyone's hands. The small, sweet creature who wore those tiny pink gloves and her smile could make everyone happy.

Ralph covered Shania's face with her tiny, pink hat and hid her in his hug while he took a few more steps to come closer to the truth. He walked toward the woman who was talking to the cats and seemed lost and scared.

"Ralph…" Mrs. Pears whispered.

Now it was his turn to find out if his instincts were right. He couldn't deal with his mother's guessing. His heart was beating faster and faster, while his footsteps continued driving them toward her side. At the same time, his mother remained silent and began caressing his back.

"Take it easy, honey." his mother said.

The moment Ralph stood in front of the woman and saw her eyes, he was taken aback. There was no way to forget her big, blue eyes. In a flash he locked his eyes on hers while his mother took the baby in her arms. Ralph went closer to the mysterious woman while his thoughts kept fighting against his fears. There was no way to forget her long, blonde hair and her sweet face.

Mrs. Pears had only seen her two times, and she recognized her immediately. She would never forget her look and her sorrowful eyes.

"Hi," Ralph said hesitantly.

Although they were both in their early twenties, she looked tired and older than her age.

"Hi," the tall woman said softly.

Mrs. Pears smiled at her and then she looked toward her son and caught his hand.

"I am going to have a walk," she said and squeezed Shania in her arms, smiling at the young couple. "It was nice to meet you."

"What are you doing here?" Ralph asked, gazing at the woman who had stolen his heart and his mind.

"I'm scolding my cats. They never listen to me!" she exclaimed.

Ralph was staring at his partner in silence and he didn't know what to do. He kept looking at Sonya, unable to react. He swept away the tears of uncertainty, his mind in turmoil, he thought, *What happened to my beloved partner?*

The woman in front of him was weak, helpless, seeking for support, for medical help. It was obvious that she had experienced a nervous breakdown since she had no contact with reality.

Ralph could never imagine that he would meet

Sonya again under these circumstances. He was used to seeing a beautiful, confident woman and now the sight of this lady made him freeze. His partner needed his help, she needed someone to lift her up and give her life back. Sonya seemed exhausted and could hardly walk or move her hands. Her gloves were wet, the wrinkles around her eyes and her messy hair showed off her physical and emotional deterioration.

"I see," Ralph said kindly. The only thing he wanted was to take her back home and help her overcome her troubles.

For the last forty-eight hours Sonya had been homeless. Her clothes were dirty; her coat was covered with mud. Her shoes were soaked.

Sonya was stranded in the zone of nothing due to the pressure she had experienced and, unfortunately, Ralph was not aware of her situation. He had realized that she was distant and hesitant to speak up, but he thought that her behavior was the result of her fatigue during the nine months of her pregnancy.

"How long have you been here?" Ralph asked, squeezing his fingers in the pockets of his jacket.

"I have no idea," his partner mumbled, shaking her head.

"What's your name?" Ralph asked and looked into her eyes. He was still shocked, but he had to find out how her breakdown had affected her memory.

"Sonya," she answered.

"Do you know who am I? Do you know my name?" he asked and bit his lips, waiting patiently for her answer.

"Ralph!" Sonya cried out.

Suddenly, all the pain, the horrible, unanswered questions along with the tears of their short separation disappeared. It was obvious that Sonya was the one who was seeking for Ralph while he was not there for her. If only she had told him everything concerning her worries and had revealed the dark secrets in her mind.

Unfortunately, Ralph had no idea what was going on in his partner's mind. If she had mentioned the facts that she wanted to bury, Sonya would have been his priority. Now, Ralph was flirting with an *a priori* situation and he couldn't waste his time. He had to save his partner, the mother of his child.

Watching the woman he was crazy in love in that situation was the most startling experience of his entire life. But he would never do that mistake; Sonya would never feel helpless again. If only she knew how much he loved her.

"Do your cats have names?" Ralph asked.

"Of course they have names," Sonya smiled and pointed at the first cat, which was near her shoes.

Ralph brushed the snow from the wooden bench and then they sat down and continued talking about the cats. After a while, Mrs. Pears and Shania joined their company and the middle-aged woman looked curious about Sonya's reaction. Ralph waited to see if Sonya would say something to her daughter, but his partner said nothing. Instead, she started crying.

"I think I should go home with the baby," Mrs. Pears said, and her son nodded at her.

Ralph held Sonya's hands and they played with the colorful kitties, laughing like the old days.

"Everything will be fine," he said.

When Ralph saw Sonya's pained smile, he was sure that things would change. The insecurities were gone. *Can't let go*, he thought and then he stretched out his arm and offered his hand.

"What?" Sonya wondered.

"Let's go home," Ralph said and Sonya followed him.

Chapter Ten

Five months later, everything had changed.

***

When Ralph returned back home and saw Sonya playing with Shania, he smiled and waved at them, calling out his daughter's name. They were strolling outside the house near the garage while their four cats were lying on the grass watching their steps, waiting for their touch.

The moment Ralph saw their smiles, he felt the happiest man on earth since his partner was healthy and his daughter had gotten her mother back. Shania would never be alone again because Sonya was there, he was there, and they would always be next to her side.

"Ddd…" his daughter wanted to speak up, but it was too early. She looked angry, she was disappointed, but her father loved the way she was trying to make those incredible sounds, which could turn a bad day at work into the most interesting experience in his life. Ralph was impatient to hear his daughter calling out for him.

Superdad—yes, that would be perfect, he thought, and he laughed.

He took a few steps and stood next to his family. Ralph could see that Sonya was truly happy; she was focused on her recovery while she was interested in doing her best for their family's harmony as well.

Sonya hugged him and smiled tearfully. Ralph saw her tears running down her beautiful, sweet face and held her tight. He was waiting for this moment for too long and, now, he was ready to celebrate the fact that the nightmare was finally over. That day would become the happiest one of his entire life.

He had done everything the doctors had told him and he was determined to keep on following their suggestions. He would never press Sonya again and he would insist on learning everything that would bother her.

During her therapy, doctors had mentioned many times that Sonya shouldn't be distracted by Ralph's feelings and the needs of their baby. Sonya needed time, they both needed time, and Ralph fought for both of them against all the difficulties while taking care of their baby. He wanted to see his partner becoming strong and positive again, and he was sure that she would win this battle.

"I love you," Sonya stared at him and smiled.

"I love you too," he said and kissed her lips.

Shania was watching them. She seemed the happiest girl and so did Sonya.

"What are you looking at?" Ralph said and kissed his daughter's forehead.

He knelt and took her in his arms; he locked his daughter in his hug and held her mother's hand tight. Then, they started dancing and laughing. Their daughter was thrilled. She kept laughing and waving her hands.

Ralph experienced absolute pleasure and he loved gazing at them as they both looked wonderful. Their long, yellow dresses and their blonde hair made them look like the most adorable mother and daughter in the world. He couldn't find the appropriate words to describe their facial expressions, but he was certain that their smiles would seal every cell of his mind forever. Euphoria, kindness, and love flooded his soul as he was sure he didn't miss anything.

"I almost forgot," he whispered and placed his daughter on the grass.

"What is it?" Sonya asked. She was surprised, but she also knew the kind of man she had decided to have in her life.

"I brought you something," Ralph said.

He went back to the car and she watched him, curious about his surprise. He had decided to make things like the way they used to be.

"Ice cream!" she said with a little laugh.

"I know that you love it," he said.

"White chocolate?" Sonya asked, sounding like a little girl.

"Of course!" Ralph grinned.

They enjoyed the ice cream and laughed and played together. They were happy, indeed.

Chapter Eleven

A s he was looking at the ceiling of the baby's room, he heard his partner's footsteps. Ralph was sitting in the chair and felt wonderful as he could hear his daughter breathing peacefully, and that was the best sound he had ever heard. Then again, the presence of his partner in their home had changed his mood entirely and he had started making dreams for the future again.

Before long, Sonya stood next to the pink door of their daughter's room and smiled at him. She was so beautiful that he couldn't take his eyes off her. The way she gazed at him triggered his secret desires and woke up his physical needs. He wanted to feel her body on his. Ralph never stopped being in love with his partner, and he had already forgiven her.

"I missed you so much, Ralph," she whispered.

"I missed you too, baby." he said as he walked to her.

They closed the door of their bedroom and made love and sensed euphoria running in their veins. They couldn't stop caressing and kissing one another's body.

After so many months, their time had finally come and it was wonderful smelling and touching and giving pleasure to each other.

Although Ralph couldn't wait for their private moments, he refrained from demanding attention since he was told to be cautious and patient. As expected, he did nothing but wait. Ralph would never risk doing something wrong; he would never endanger his partner's health.

"Every time you need me, I'll be here," Ralph whispered, looking into her eyes.

"Now you know everything. I'm sorry I lied to you about my family," Sonya murmured avoiding his gaze in an effort to apologize.

Ralph kissed her lips and smiled at her. It was not

the time to get all the answers he looked for yet, and although he had no intention to make his partner upset, he had to know.

"That's fine, baby. I just want to know what happened to you."

"I have no idea, Ralph."

Sonya caressed his face and he half-closed his eyes. He had missed that touch and the feelings it caused to his soul. He was relieved, he loved smelling her perfume and lying in bed with her.

"Your brother will never hurt you again. He is in Europe."

"I know that."

"Now tell me, how are you?" he asked and looked forward to hearing her answer.

"I'm fine. I promise I will never do it again." Sonya sounded guilty, like a little a girl who had done something bad and waited for her punishment.

"Are you happy with me?" Ralph asked again.

"You are the best man of all. You are my angel," she said.

Sonya kissed her partner and then she started teasing him since, after a while, she began searching all over his body and his head.

"What are you doing?" he asked nervously.

"I'm searching for your halo!" Sonya said with a little laugh.

"What?" Ralph kept smiling.

"I'm so sorry for everything," she said and lay on his chest.

"I will always be there for you," Ralph answered and he was there for his partner, protecting her in his embrace.

"I love you, Ralph."

"I love you too, Sonya."

He kissed his partner and caressed her hair and,

now, he was sure that she would never leave their home again.

Sonya was healthy. During her therapy, she never refused medication because she really wanted to overcome the games of her mind and her dangerous disease.

"Will you marry me?" Ralph proposed. The moment he showed her the ring, his partner couldn't hide her enthusiasm and joy. The tears of happiness started running down her beautiful face.

"I thought you didn't believe in marriage," she managed to say.

"I was wrong. Now, I do believe. Will you marry me?" he asked again.

"Yes!" she exclaimed joyfully. He kissed her and caressed her beautiful hair, promising to stand by her side forever. He would always protect his family and take care of his wife.

The moment Sonya kissed him, Ralph felt his soul coming closer to heaven. He had found his lost angel again and he was grateful to God.

Chapter Twelve

"And now they are up there," the aged woman whispered and looked upon the sky.

"Dad loved Mom," Ryan said.

"Yes, he really loved your mother," the woman admitted.

Shania remained silent, watching the surface of the water. The heat and the memories of her parents made her feel despaired, and she wanted to escape. She needed to come back to life and the cold water could be the best way to move on.

Shania got up from the chair and dived into the pool. She swam toward the other side of the pool and avoided looking back. Her grandma knew and she was also sure that Shania needed time to adjust to reality and life. And she would make it--she just needed time.

The aged woman caressed Ryan's face and they headed toward the beautiful garden. It was the time to make plans for the night.

"Will they be together forever?" Ryan asked and gazed upon his grandma.

"Yes, honey. They will be together forever."

She looked down at her grandchild and smiled. She would never overcome the loss of her son and his wife. She would never forget the terrible accident. The plane crashed into the ocean, Ralph and Sonya never came back home from London. They were supposed to have fun and travel across Europe, but fate had other plans. At least they were together, never to be apart again.

~END~

Courage, sacrifice, determination, commitment, toughness, heart, talent, guts. That's what little girls are made of.
Bethany Hamilton

Can't Let Go: Afterword

W hen Sonya gave birth to their baby, she thought she had lost her youth. Sonya believed she was not able to handle the entire situation. She was suffering from depression and Ralph hadn't realized that it could actually cost her life.

The first days of their return from the hospital Sonya couldn't sleep and she stopped eating. Pretty soon she found it difficult to take care of herself. She was all the time next to the baby neglecting the rest things, ignoring her needs, ignoring her own health.

Then again, her brother's appearance was destructive. When Sonya kicked him out of the house, she opened the envelope and read everything concerning her mother's medical condition and, furthermore, she had the chance to get some more information about her mother's pregnancy and the unknown father that no one had ever mentioned to her.

Sonya couldn't believe that her mother was mentally sick and couldn't accept the fact that Erica had betrayed Aston and, additionally, all of them as well. Erica had made her daughter hate the only man who loved her and always supported her actions, causing Sonya the worst pain she had ever felt in her heart.

Aston, the best man Sonya had met, had never cheated on her mother, but it was too late to say sorry and to thank him for all those he had done to see her happy. Aston was the man she had met as her father and she would never be able to ask some questions about her mother's condition. Sonya would never accept her mother's duplicity.

Erica had no contact with reality, she had refused medication and, after a few months, she killed herself. She had said so many lies to her daughter about Aston and she was sure and happy as well that Sonya would never like him. Moreover, Erica had never told anyone the truth about Sonya's father in order to protect her daughter's feelings and to seal the safe environment Aston was eager to offer her.

As for John, he was suffocated and he wanted to reveal everything to his sister because he waited for many years to hurt her. John hated Sonya, he regarded that his sister was behaving like a spoiled child who had never respected his father and everything he had done for her.

John hated his mother too since she had never been the mother he wished for. He felt embarrassed introducing his mother to his friends and he felt sorry for his father for tolerating a woman who deserved nothing but abandonment. Although Aston had begged him not to say anything to Sonya -because he had predicted the disappointment her mother's betrayal would cause her and he wanted to protect her since he really loved her- he didn't keep his promise to his father.

When Sonya heard her brother's words, she couldn't handle all the pressure. She wanted to get away and she really needed to have some time to find herself, ignoring the fact that she had a baby and a lovely partner.

After her adventure, Sonya admitted that she didn't know what she had done and that she wasn't able to think of her family. Later, they discovered that she was sleeping in a church and she was safe in God's hands. Sonya was fighting for her survival and she made it.

About the Author:

As a child, A.A dreamed of being a cardiac surgeon. Later, Schenna realized that this was not what he wanted.

Writing has always been his greatest pleasure. When he doesn't write action, adventure, romance stories or anything else, he reads everything.

Schenna admires all the writers he comes across and enjoys talking about books and magazines.

A.A loves meeting new people and discovering new places.

Trapped in Timelessness, Lake's Curse, The Alphas, Limitless Love Collection, On the Sixth Floor are available through the Solstice Publishing website.

Acknowledgements:

In gratitude for the careful guidance my new career has received over the past two years:
To my dear editor-in-chief and good friend K.C Sprayberry, thank you for believing in me.
A sincere thank you to my friends at Solstice Publishing who helped me promote my work and get my books out there.
Thank you, Nick and Jim.
A big thank you to Cynthia Ley, my editor at Solstice Publishing.

Social Media Links:

Website: www.aaschenna.com

Facebook: https://www.facebook.com/pages/AA-Schenna/701740166542505?ref=hl

Twitter: https://twitter.com/ASchenna

Other Work by A.A. Schenna

Limitless Love Collection:

Three stories of romance for lovers of all ages.

On The Sixth Floor:

Jenna never thought she would run into true love. Will John be the exception to her rule?

Trapped In Timelessness:

"When Brittany saw the beast running toward his side, she started screaming."
The chemistry teacher couldn't stand staring at the nasty, bloody creature. She was only interested in her beloved partner, her Bruce.
The moment the four teenagers heard the mysterious man's confession, they were ready to give up. For a while, the silence made their minds walk on the paths of the past. If only they knew the way to go back home.
The carefree stroll in the woods managed to trap them in timelessness. The four students along with their teachers would have to deal with an absurd fate.
The red scorpions, the large eagles, the nasty bats, and the bloody creatures were determined to haunt them forever.

The moment they came across the craziest adventure of their lives, they would have to struggle to survive.

Trapped In Timelessness: Lake's Curse:

Green Lake was a beautiful place any time of year. A beautiful place where ten people disappeared every century at the end of a muddy rope.

On the verge of graduation, Nick and Leona knew nothing of this. It wasn't until the nightmare came for them that the curse became real, and their futures changed far beyond what they could ever have dreamed.

Trapped In Timelessness: Black Angels:

The black angels have come, destroying the world to remake it in their own image. Some humans will survive, even overcome. As their world burns, they will rise from the ashes.

And some survivors will fall.

Trapped In Timelessness: Fallen Angels:

The carefree stroll in the woods managed to trap them in timelessness. The four students along with their teachers would have to deal with an absurd fate.
The red scorpions, the large eagles, the nasty bats, and the bloody creatures were determined to haunt them forever.
The moment they came across the craziest adventure of their lives, they would have to struggle to survive.
***
Green Lake was a beautiful place any time of year, a beautiful place where ten people disappeared every century

at the end of a muddy rope.

On the verge of graduation, Nick and Leona knew nothing of this. It wasn't until the nightmare came for them that the curse became real, and their futures changed far beyond what they could ever have dreamed.

***

The black angels have come, destroying the world to remake it in their own image. Some humans will survive, even overcome. As their world burns, they will rise from the ashes.

www.ingramcontent.com/pod-product-compliance
Lightning Source LLC
Chambersburg PA
CBHW070605180626
46817CB00005B/2009